"I ALWAYS LOVED THE WAY YOU TASTED," SHE MURMURED, HER BREATH HOT AGAINST HIS SKIN.

Restraint snapped, dissolved in a rush of need to touch Claire's skin. He tugged the hem of her knit blouse from inside her jeans and peeled off the top.

Claire's full breasts strained against the pink lace of a skimpy bra. Only a delicate front closure held the garment against her body.

Hands trembling, he released the hook and her breasts fell free of their constraint.

Claire hooked her thumbs beneath the straps and, arching her back, slid it up over her head. With a snap of her hand, the lingerie sailed somewhere to the floor. Dugan didn't care where. He only knew he lifted heaven in his hands, Claire's silky breasts.

While Dugan pleasured himself, she dispensed with his shirt and let it slide from her fingers over the side of the bed. She threw her head back and moaned at the exquisite aching his circling thumbs brought to her distended nipples. As she straddled Dugan's abdomen, insistent contractions seized her there between her thighs.

"Ah, Claire, why did we wait so long?"

"We waited so it could be like this. As good as before." She bent to flick his skin with her tongue. "No, better."

NANCY BERLAND

Ties That Bind

ZEBRA BOOKS
KENSINGTON PUBLISHING CORP.

ZEBRA BOOKS

are published by

Kensington Publishing Corp.
475 Park Avenue South
New York, NY 10016

First printing: October, 1992

Printed in the United States of America

For Alice Orr
Agent, Mentor, Friend

ACKNOWLEDGMENTS

Thanks to Dr. Roger Johnson, for sharing both his passion for his profession and his experiences as the only doctor in a small Texas town;

To Jane and Scott Johnson, the gracious proprietors of Hotel Turkey, Turkey, Texas, for their southern hospitality while they educated this author on the beauty of their West Texas region,

And to Marcie Gardenhire, who has lovingly prepared many a mom for natural childbirth and who provided the realistic detail for Pamela Sue's labor.

Prologue

"I must be dreaming," Claire mumbled. "Run that one by me again."

"I said, the town council floated a bond issue to build a two-million-dollar clinic," Claire's Aunt Lila repeated in the gentile West Texas accent that spoke of home. "And they're looking for a doctor to run it."

"You want me to pass the word around up here?"

"Claire, Claire, where are your brains? I want *you* to apply!"

Claire tossed her wrinkled lab coat into the hamper and flopped back onto the lumpy sleeper couch in her efficiency apartment. After walking six blocks in a mid-May East Coast steam bath, she'd trudged up three flights of stairs glaze-eyed to find her telephone ringing. It was a long distance call from Sierra, Texas.

As a third-year resident in a mammoth Philadelphia hospital, Claire had just completed another exhausting stint. She could barely summon the energy to talk, much less make sense out of the proposition her great aunt was making.

"Aunt Lila, you know how I feel about going back to Sierra."

"What if I told you the job'll pay a big, fat salary?"

"Not good enough. You see, I've already — "

"And Sierra'll pay the doctor's malpractice insurance premiums."

"Wow! That's some incentive. Still, I — "

"The building's almost finished. We've ordered X-ray equipment, and an electrocardiograph, and the prettiest carpet you've ever seen."

Claire leaned back against the comfort of the cushions and closed her eyes. "That all sounds wonderful, Aunt Lila, but I'm so tired, I can't see straight. Let me catch a couple hours' sleep, and I'll call you back."

"Don't you hang up on me, Claire Linwood. You hear? Not when I'm offerin' you the chance to have that clinic you've dreamed of since you were knee-high to a grasshopper."

Claire felt herself slipping into the blessed oblivion of sleep while her aunt continued her lecture. But something Lila said yanked Claire from the rest her body craved.

". . . and the best part is, if you stick around Sierra for five years, you'll get half ownership of the clinic."

Claire's eyes snapped open. "Half? Are you serious?"

"Serious as sin. Now are you interested?"

"Well . . ."

"Good. Now listen to your aunt. Got a pencil?"

"Somewhere around here."

Claire found a worn-down stub under the couch cushion in time to jot down a number her Aunt Lila rattled off.

"That's the phone at Harvey Winthrop's hardware store. Fix up a resumé and fax it to me — quick now. I've got to have it by Monday. And don't forget all the good stuff, like those high marks you made on the family practice exam. I'll let you know when the board decides to do the interviewin'."

"Who's on the board?"

"Me for one."

"That's convenient."

"So right off, you've got one vote."

"Who else?"

"Oh, the usual — Harvey, and Orville Garrison. You remember Orville, don't you?"

Did she! The thought of his cocky grin made Claire's tired blood boil, even after all these years. Orville was the tight-fisted president of Sierra's only bank. He single-handedly decided whose dreams came true and whose didn't. "Anyone else I know?"

"Two or three. How soon you figure you could get away for an interview?"

"I finish my residency in two weeks." *If I live that long,* Claire thought. "But, as I was trying to tell you earlier, I'm already committed. I accepted a position with a group practice here in Philadelphia."

"Two weeks'll do, but no later," Lila commented, as if Claire's job didn't exist. "I'll send you an ap-

11

plication and a copy of the contract. Gives me goose bumps just thinkin' you might come back home to Sierra."

Back home to Sierra. In her weakened state, the reality of what Claire was considering hit her like a well-placed blow to the solar plexus. Sierra was the last place she wanted to establish a medical practice. Located east of the Palo Duro Canyon, the town had never managed to exceed population six hundred. But that had nothing to do with her reluctance to settle there. She actually preferred the more relaxed, small-town life-style.

What she didn't like were the gut-wrenching memories of her last two years in Sierra. Especially that morning twelve years ago. Dugan Nichols had stuffed her and a banged-up suitcase onto a bus, without so much as a hint of remorse or a farewell kiss for his young wife. Claire had cried half the way to Philadelphia and her Aunt Sophie's boarding house. When the crying was done, Claire had sworn she would never go back as long as Dugan lived there.

Still, the bait Lila was dangling was too tempting to ignore. Few doctors straight out of residency had the opportunity Sierra was offering. Maybe Dugan had moved.

"Is *he* still there?" she asked her aunt.

"I can't imagine who you're referrin' to."

"Aunt Lila, I'm too tired to play games. You know who I mean."

"If you mean Dugan, yes, the man has chosen to stick around."

Dugan. Spoken out loud, his name conjured up painful memories. How could she think of going home if he was there, a constant reminder of more heartache than any woman should be forced to endure?

"If Dugan's still there, it's out of the question," she maintained.

"I can't believe you'd let that poor excuse for a *man* — and I use the term loosely — destroy the chance of a lifetime. You'd be a rich lady in five years. If you pass up that chance, I'll guaran-damn-tee you, Claire Linwood, you'll regret it for the rest of your years."

Chapter One

Nothing had changed.

The dry June wind still whipped through Sierra, flinging sand from the loamy soil through closed windows and doorways and threatening to steal Claire's breath.

Outside the town's only bank, in a narrow slice of shade, Ebert Morgan sat on a weathered bench at high noon. As he had for years, Ebert whittled miniature farm animals with his ivory-handled knife.

And, try though she might to subdue it, Claire's heart still fluttered at the thought that only ten miles east was Dugan Nichols. He'd be sitting proudly atop his Appaloosa or his run-down tractor, working what was left of the pitiful acreage his great grandfather had homesteaded.

She could almost see the sweat glistening on Dugan's bronzed chest, feel the hard muscles that dipped into his butt-hugging jeans, feel the power of thighs that had pressed into hers before Angela had blessed their bleak lives for a few precious hours.

Angela. As Claire whispered her name, the warm, dry wind snatched it from her lips. With a masterful effort, she fought off the tears that accompanied a dizzying wave of nostalgia. Two minutes in Sierra, and the ache in her chest was almost more than she could bear.

When she'd left Philadelphia, Claire had promised herself she wouldn't let the memories back home torture her. She would apply the detachment she'd learned at medical school to emotions long denied. Physically, she was a mature, healthy woman now. That much had changed, thanks to time and Aunt Sophie. And Claire was a doctor. She ought to be able to heal the wounds gaping open in her heart.

Memories or no memories, if she persuaded the board to choose a native daughter over the other applicants, she could have a dream clinic. She could practice medicine the way a doctor was meant to practice. One on one, and to hell with the dictates of Medicare bureaucrats and health insurance companies. According to the terms of the proposed contract tucked into Claire's briefcase, the clinic's doctor was never to turn away a local patient who couldn't afford treatment.

She would simply have to slip those old memories . . . old hurts . . . into a remote closet of her mind and forget them.

A streak of brown-gold sand smudged her starched linen blouse as she popped the trunk of her rental car. So much for a professional appearance, she thought, and reached inside for her suitcase and medical bag.

"My word—Claire! I wasn't expectin' you till mornin'."

At the sound of Lila's voice, Claire swung around and embraced the bright-eyed widow, who still wore a pencil stuck sideways through a thick silver bun. "One night in Amarillo was enough for me. All my old friends have moved away. I decided to drive on in. I couldn't wait to smell fresh air and see—"

"The clinic."

"And you." Claire stole a wayward glance down the road leading east of town before adding, "You look well."

"Clean livin' and a glass of wine before bed," Lila responded with a playful chuckle. "Well, let's get you out of this dang-blasted wind and grit, or you'll be needin' to doctor yourself."

Claire's aunt, who at seventy-two was as sturdy as most women half her age, stuck her thumb and forefinger between her lips and gave a shrill whistle. A head popped into view in the window of Sierra's only hotel, a two-story edifice built in 1927 but restored since Claire had left.

"That Fred! Still as lazy as a nursin' sow," Lila grumbled. She motioned for the hotel's long-standing bell hop and handyman to fetch Claire's suitcase from the car's trunk.

"Fred," Claire murmured and prepared for a hug she sorely needed. She could hardly wait to feel his comforting arms about her.

But she took one look at his weathered, whiskered face, his impassive expression, and her smile faded. She watched him tip his straw hat solicitously and hoist her suitcase from the car's trunk with a complaining groan. Without so much as a backward glance, he left her standing by her car, the sand swirling at her feet and need nipping at her heart.

Where was the welcoming embrace from the man she'd loved like an uncle? From the man who'd given away her hand in marriage after her parents had died within six weeks of each other when she was a senior in high school?

Her last recollection of Fred flashed before her eyes. When Claire had left Sierra twelve years ago, as a frail and heartbroken twenty-year-old, he had told her he'd always be there for her. Now he regarded her as if she were a stranger—and an unwelcome one at that.

Sierra folks didn't treat strangers that rudely, much less one of their own. At least she hadn't witnessed such blatant lack of manners during her years there.

Was it conceivable Dugan had spread lies about her after she'd left to justify what he'd done to break her heart? To explain a departure so hasty there hadn't been time for the church circle to honor her with a farewell social?

Claire glanced around the nearly deserted block, one of six in the modest business district. Despite the warm June air, a shiver worked its way up her spine. She could almost feel curious eyes studying her from behind store windows. Would others be as

18

hostile as Fred? And if so, why? She'd done nothing wrong, unless—

"This all, *Doc* Linwood?" Fred asked curtly over his shoulder.

"Yes," she answered, still puzzled by his hostile attitude. "And please, call me Claire, like old times." Moving up beside him, she patted him affectionately on the back and gave his aging shoulder a gentle squeeze. "I may be a doctor now, but I'm still the same Claire who used to beg you for piggyback rides."

Even though she gave Fred her warmest smile, he appeared to ignore her entreaty. He harrumped loudly as he maneuvered the suitcase up the stairs and into the lobby of the hotel. In a good month, the place counted more guests staying in its twenty rooms than the town counted residents.

As she and her aunt followed Fred, Claire thought of the times he'd held her on his lap and regaled her with stories of his growing-up years as a scamp. In those days before the Depression the town elders were sure the railroad's arrival would turn Sierra into a bustling center of commerce.

An aching lump grew in her throat. She crossed her arms over the hollowness in her stomach. Why couldn't Fred offer her the comfort of a welcoming hug?

"We'll get you settled, then grab a bite to eat at Imogene's," Lila said while frowning in Fred's direction. "Can't have you missin' any meals."

"That's all in the past, Aunt Lila. Besides, I'd rather see the clinic first."

19

"After you eat, my dear. Plenty of time to see the clinic before your interview in the mornin'."

Now that Claire had survived her arrival with her emotions frayed, yet intact for the most part, she realized how much she wanted the job. As her own boss, she could determine policy. No more bureaucratic red tape that had shackled her in that Philadelphia hospital where she'd conducted her residency. No more thou-shalt-nots because what was best for the patient wasn't financially lucrative for the hospital. No more refusals to permit her to do the work she was trained to do — practice family medicine.

Yes, ironically, here in Sierra she could find the answer to her dreams, if she could ignore the source of her worst nightmares ten miles east of town, down a dirt road.

And that, as Lila would say, was a mighty big if.

"How do you read the board?" Claire asked her. "You think they want me?" She tipped an indifferent Fred two dollars and closed the door behind him. "If he's any example of the welcome I can expect, we both may be in for a disappointment."

"Hogwash. They want you. You'll see," Lila replied. Yet she deftly avoided Claire's gaze by shuffling clothes from suitcase to closet in the quaint room that overlooked Main Street.

"The way I figure it," Claire said, "the package the town's offering is worth well over two million dollars."

"Closer to three, if you tack on the malpractice insurance premiums."

20

"How many applied? Fifty? A hundred?"

"Nope. Just the seven."

"Only seven? Why?"

"You're forgettin' we aren't much more'n a wide place in the road. Culture's a bit lackin'. Besides, as I'm sure you know, lots of towns like Sierra filled the bill by payin' for a doctor's expenses through medical school. We're Johnny-come-latelies, and the pickin's are slim."

"Still . . ."

"Since you left, we've had our fill of highfalutin' doctors. Had a few years' city practice on 'em, and acted like Sierra was a pit somebody dumped 'em in. They'd stick around six months, a year maybe, and—" she snapped her fingers and her kind blue eyes fairly bristled "—they'd move on to greener pastures, so to speak. The board decided to stick with folks committed to small-town livin'." She tweaked Claire's cheek. "People like my pretty little niece here."

"I would prefer a small-town practice," she admitted, "but I'm puzzled about something."

"What's that?"

"Fred. He sure behaved strangely."

"Never you mind that old fool."

"But we were so close."

"Twelve years ago. And you will be again. Give folks a chance to get reacquainted. They'll warm to you in no time."

"Not everyone will, and you know it."

Lila brushed an unruly lock of Claire's golden hair from her eyes. "We'll have to do somethin' about your hair. A doctor can't have a mane as wild as a stallion's."

"Aunt Lila, you still have that maddening habit of changing the subject whenever it suits you."

"Okay, so maybe not everyone will greet you with say hey and open arms."

"Is he well?" Claire couldn't help asking, a telltale catch to her voice.

"I can't believe you're askin' after that man."

"Is he?" Claire persisted.

Her aunt shrugged. "Was last time I saw him."

"Which was when?"

"Saturday mornin'. Brought lettuce into market."

"Did he ever marry?"

"Course not. No one'd have him."

"Then is he — ?"

"Engaged? Nope. And he isn't goin' with anyone. Dates once a month or so. Some birdbrained redhead from Amarillo. Lord a mercy, Claire. Don't tell me you're still harborin' feelin's for the man after what he gone and done to you."

"I have no intentions of ever seeing him again, if that's what you mean."

"As the only doctor in town, you'd have to see him, if he's ailin'."

"Of course I'd see him, like anybody else. What I meant was I'll never let Dugan Nichols worm his way into my heart again."

"And pigs fly," Lila grumbled under her breath. "Maybe this wasn't such a good idea after all."

Claire crossed to the window, which was draped with swags of polished cotton in a splashy floral

22

print. Drawing aside the Victorian lace panel, she surveyed the town. It was here that she'd grown up as the carefree daughter of Ben and Alice Linwood, teachers at the school that served three towns.

By now a few old-timers were drifting out of Imogene Parker's Good Eatin' Cafe. She recognized Orville Garrison by his swagger and his shiny bald pate. The years had salted the bank president's hair a few shades grayer and swelled the paunch that lapped over his tightly cinched belt.

And there was Moses Keller, the owner of Sierra's car repair shop/service station/new and used book store. Claire wondered if Moses had developed a mind of his own or if he still followed Orville around like an obedient pup.

The screen door to the cafe swung open. A tall, lean cowboy in faded blue jeans as tight as skin stepped into the West Texas sun. He swept off his straw cowboy hat and wiped the sand and perspiration from his brow with the sleeve of his sky-blue shirt. The sun reflected off jet black hair that, waving over his shirt collar, was long overdue for a cut.

Dugan. Claire pressed her hand to her lips to keep it from trembling. She could still feel the thick, lustrous texture of his hair between her fingers. To save money, she used to tie an old checkered tablecloth around his neck and trim his shaggy locks.

Once, to persuade him to make time for the task, she had locked her legs around his waist and started snipping while she rubbed her bare breasts against his back. Before she finished, he grabbed the scissors and slung them out of reach. They made love

23

on the floor beside the claw-footed bathtub. Afterward, they climbed inside and took turns soaping each other in slow, deliberate strokes. Later Dugan's buddies had teased him about his lop-sided haircut.

Claire knew she should back away from the window and lock the self-destructive memories from her mind. Still, she couldn't tear her gaze from the man who had told her he didn't love her anymore. The man who had ripped her ailing heart into shreds when he'd sent her away to Philadelphia.

He lifted the sole of one foot to his knee and scraped what looked like a wad of pink gum from his cowboy boot. Although the black boots were caked with dust, she recognized them with a painful stab to her chest. They were the same ones he'd worn, polished to a high sheen, to their June wedding after they'd graduated from high school.

He glanced across the street, his gaze lighting on the rental car Claire had driven the ninety minutes from Amarillo. He frowned at the white sedan that was the only car on the street with an out-of-county tag.

He ambled down the steps of the sidewalk onto the asphalt street. The bank president said something to him, and Dugan's movements stilled. His gaze shot straight to the hotel's second story and collided with Claire's. The force couldn't have been any greater if he'd lobbed a softball into her face. The pain swept over her in undulating waves. A faint whimper slipped from her lips.

Why couldn't she release the lace folds from her hand, ignore the skittering beat of her heart? *Be-*

cause, you fool, you've wondered too many years how you'd feel if you ever saw Dugan again. Now that you know, the wondering's over.

He tipped his hat at her. That lazy, dimpled smile that had always turned her insides to jelly creased his sun-baked face. One cold December day after lunch he'd lured her from the kitchen into the bedroom with that seductive grin. Her pot of stew had burned so bad Lazy Boy, their hound dog, had taken one whiff of it and backed away from his bowl.

For three evenings straight she and Dugan had eaten canned beans, but not once had he complained. He'd merely winked at her over his bowl and stuffed a piece of cornbread in his mouth in such a manner that she would have done anything for one more chance to make love with him.

Why the grin now? she thought with a sudden flash of resentment. Why not twelve years ago when she would have traded her soul for one smile, one final loving touch from her husband?

She whirled away from the window and found her aunt watching her with a disapproving scowl.

"Stop that," she told Lila.

"Stop what?"

"Looking at me as if I didn't have an ounce of sense in my head."

"My dear, if the shoe fits—"

"Because," Claire interrupted her, "it'll be a cold day in hell before I let Dugan get close enough to hurt me again."

* * *

25

Claire looked better than Imogene Parker's lemon meringue pie. And if Dugan's memory served him well, she tasted sweeter by far.

The taste and texture of her freshly bathed skin sprang to his mind. Jasmine and satin and blush pink — those were his recollections of Claire.

He remembered the first time he'd walked in on her in the bathroom. She'd been such a shy thing, scooching down so the bubbles covered her breasts. But he'd patiently coaxed her with tender kisses until she slowly emerged from the water, iridescent bubbles sliding down over her perky breasts and her taut stomach into the juncture of her thighs. While she'd watched with heavy-lidded eyes, he'd quickly shed his clothes and joined her in the tub.

Afterward, they had laughed over the eight towels they'd used to mop up all the soapy water that had sloshed over the side.

Another vision crowded the first from his memory. The vacant, questioning look in her eyes as he'd forced her onto that bus to Philadelphia without so much as a peck on the cheek from him. Sending her away had been the most difficult thing he'd ever done in his life.

He watched her drop the window curtain as if it were a hot coal. A hard knot twisted in his gut.

What did you expect, after what you did, old boy? A welcome with open arms?

He said his farewells to Orville and Moses and crossed the street to fetch his new pickup from the garage mechanic. He thought of Ruby, the broken-down truck still parked behind his sprawling new

26

ranch house. The old girl was peeling orange-red paint into the weedy soil beneath her rusty frame.

He hadn't been able to part with Ruby. Even now, after twelve years, he could sit in her, close his eyes and remember the good times with Claire. Remember their first date. Remember the first time they'd made love, two years later, lying on a blanket beside Ruby in Joseph Witcomb's north forty.

Sometimes, when the winds stilled, Dugan would sit in Old Ruby and capture the clean, floral scent that had been uniquely Claire's. He'd run his hands over the tattered upholstery and remember how silky her golden thighs had felt beneath the palm of his hand as they drove into town for what store-bought supplies they could afford.

Right now sunflowers were pushing through the rusted-out holes in the truck bed. A brood of rabbits had burrowed into the ground beneath the cab.

A brood of rabbits—the ultimate irony, he thought with a remorseful shake of his head.

If he could persuade Claire to see him again—hell, to talk to him even—maybe he could make her understand what had driven him to send her away. But until the clinic's board chose the doctor, he did not dare sit down with her for so much as a cup of coffee.

Cursing, he paid Moses' mechanic for the oil change and revved up the truck's engine. In the rear-view mirror he caught Claire and her aunt strolling across the street toward Imogene's Cafe.

The fabric of Claire's mint green skirt hugged hips he'd once cupped in his eager hands. The need

27

to touch her again seized him. If he hadn't rushed lunch with the boys, he'd have been sitting in the corner booth when she walked through the door.

His first impulse was to shove the pickup in reverse and peal off backward down Main Street. He'd grab Claire and throw her in the truck, lock her inside until she listened to his reasons for hurting her the way he had.

Listen to him? Claire? Fat chance! She'd probably spit in his face before she'd let him explain the decision made by a desperate man.

Well, the doing was done. He couldn't change the past. All he could do was what he'd done for the past twelve years — take things one day at a time. If Claire saw her way clear to listen to him, fine. If not, so be it.

Chapter Two

"Well, if it ain't Claire Linwood, all growed up and citified. Long time, no see."

Claire scooted into a corner booth in the cafe, her skirt catching on a rip in the faded red vinyl. "Gunther Boone. Good to see you. How's the trapping?"

His ample backside spilling over the round counter stool, Gunther raked a beefy hand down a dense, black beard. A beard Claire figured hadn't been trimmed since she last saw him. Had the barber vacated the premises?

"Guess you forgot, being in the city and all. Trapping's out of season about now."

"Well, yes, I guess it is," Claire responded with a forced, but friendly smile.

Lila plopped a menu on the formica tabletop. "Best order before Imogene runs out of chicken fried steak."

But Gunther was like a snapping turtle who, once

he latched onto his prey, wouldn't let go until sundown. "I don't suppose those fancy folks up in Philadelphia trap much, do they?"

Before Claire could answer, Opal Sinclair slammed a chipped white porcelain mug on the counter in front of Gunther. The hot brew sloshed over the edge onto the old codger's hand.

"Ouch, woman! You done burned my shootin' hand."

"Too bad it wasn't your mouth," Opal grumbled under her breath. She shot Claire a full grin, revealing a mouthful of silver and a welcome Claire appreciated. "Glad to see you back, Claire. We've missed your pretty face. What'll it be?"

"Two chicken fried steaks, double gravy, double biscuits," Lila piped in.

"Make that one," Claire corrected her aunt. "I'll have a salad and herbal tea."

"Herbal tea," Gunther mimicked, glaring at Claire in the mirror that formed the entire back wall behind the counter. "We ain't got no herbal tea. Course if you was to go back to Philadelphia—"

Opal tipped her carafe, and more steaming hot coffee poured onto Gunther Boone's hand. "Give the girl a break. If you don't, I'll scald you all the way down to your stinking toes." Then over her shoulder she recited the order to the cook. Her colorful lingo projected Claire back in time to the once-a-month outings that hers and Dugan's limited financial resources allowed.

Gripping the wrist of his scalded hand, Gunther swore under his breath. Claire took one look at the screaming red skin and scooted out of the booth. "Here, let me see that."

Gunther jerked away from her touch and succumbed to a rattly coughing fit. "I . . . don't . . . need . . . no . . . help . . . from the likes of you," he managed to choke out.

"Opal, get Gunther a bowl of ice water. See he soaks his hand at least thirty minutes."

"Do the old coot more good if he'd soak his head," the waitress quipped, but she sauntered away in the direction of the kitchen.

"How long have you had that cough, Gunther?" Claire asked. It was deep in his chest and he didn't appear to be able to catch his breath.

"He's been like that since I can remember," Lila provided. "He's too tight to see a doctor."

"If you'll drop by the hotel this afternoon, I'll take a look at you," Claire offered.

"I ain't gonna—"

"No charge."

Gunther said nothing, only backed out the door, his face fiery red, whether from the coughing or embarrassment, Claire wasn't sure.

She turned to Lila and shook her head. "I swear. I'm beginning to wonder if coming back isn't a colossal mistake."

Something in her peripheral vision caught her attention. She turned just in time to see Dugan watching her from the sidewalk over the red gingham cafe curtains. One corner of his mouth slanted in a smile. The dimple plunged deep into his right cheek. Claire's heart plunged to the toes of her white pumps. She blinked once, and he was gone.

She moved to the window and saw him sliding into the cab of what looked like a brand new pickup truck. A part of her wanted to dart outside and intercept him before he drove away. But another, smarter part, the one that had enabled her to survive his rejection, bolted her feet to the floor.

"Too bad you had to up and leave before the times got good," Opal murmured over her shoulder. "That man of yours gone and done well for himself."

Claire whirled around. It was about time Opal — everyone in Sierra, for that matter — knew exactly why she'd left town twelve years ago. "For your information, I did not — "

"Even bought a plane," Opal went on to say. "Matter of fact, for little more than nothing he flies those that's ailing to Amarillo and Lubbock to them big hospitals. What do they call that?"

"Med-evac," Claire answered mechanically, deciding Dugan had indeed done quite well for himself once he'd rid himself of his wife.

"Best eat if you intend to take a look at the clinic," Lila said with a sudden and none-too-gentle yank on Claire's arm.

But Claire could only push the salad greens around on her plate as she measured word-for-word, glance-for-glance what had happened there in Imogene Parker's Cafe.

So that's why Fred and Gunther had treated her

as if she had a despicable infectious disease, Claire realized. They thought she had been the one to abandon Dugan.

And now that she was contemplating moving back, they were making sure she understood her return would not be heralded with the warmest of receptions.

Great. Just great, she thought bitterly the next morning. She buttoned the starched cuff of her tailored white blouse and slipped into the pale blue suit she'd carefully selected for her interview with the board. She probably had as much chance of persuading the panel to name her as the clinic's director as the drunken drifter who'd been locked up last night in the county jail.

Dugan, or no Dugan, she wanted that job, and she wouldn't let what had happened between them interfere with her chances. She'd just have to convince the board of her qualifications and her desire to come back to her hometown. God willing, she'd be happy to spend the rest of her life here.

"The rest of my life," she murmured to herself as she took the first step down the hotel's weathered oak stairs to await her turn in the parlor. She and Dugan used to play a game where he would hoist her high above his head, twirl her around and demand to know how long she'd love him. Before he would put her down, she would be coy about her answer, delighting in the dimpled grin in his uplifted face. Finally, he would tickle her, and in a fit of laughter, she'd reply, *I'll love you only for the rest of my life*.

Too bad the feeling hadn't been mutual.

Over spiced tea in the parlor, Claire met two of the other six applicants. She rather liked Doc Hardesty, an Amarillo pediatrician in his late fifties who was searching for a less demanding practice. His age, though, would work against him. The recently divorced infectious disease specialist from Chicago would undoubtedly give Claire tough competition for the post. Not only were his credentials impressive, his mid-thirties age was within the appropriate range. He was a fine-looking man with dark, Italian features and a soft-spoken manner. Sierra's ladies would adore him.

Lila poked her head around the door to the dining room. "Dr. Linwood, the board will see you now."

Claire smiled and grabbed the stack of presentation folders she'd prepared with a confidence that belied the tumbling of her stomach.

"Good luck," Lila whispered before she opened the door wide, "and try not to glare at me when you get in there."

Puzzling over her aunt's strange comment, Claire followed Lila into the dining room. From the street side the sun streamed through tall windows draped with lace sheers. On the opposite wall of the high-ceilinged room a collection of antique aprons provided a warm and friendly complement to fresh flowers on the tables.

Any other morning guests would be milling in and out of the kitchen, chatting with the hotel's gracious hostess, sitting at the cheerful tables decorated in calico blues, nursing coffee.

Today, however, the room had been reserved for

34

the board's important business. The nine members sat at a long, rectangular table with their backs to Claire, facing the interview seat, Inquisition style. Even so, she recognized Orville Garrison, the bank president, from his gleaming bald head. Besides Lila and Orville, two women and five men formed the panel that would determine her fate. Claire girded herself for what she expected would be a first-class grilling.

The moment Claire passed through the doorway, she sensed something awry. The room's air smelled of that morning's fresh biscuits and sausage despite the circulating fan fixtures overhead. Yet the atmosphere fairly crackled with tension. Claire could sense it from the stiff posture of the board members, in the whisperings of one to another.

Closer now, she studied the body language of the table's occupants one by one. Did they, like Gunther and Fred, resent her return to Sierra? Or was there something else, something she hadn't yet —

No! She stopped short. Her portfolios fell to the dense rose carpet from arms suddenly gone slack.

Dugan.

Her heart pounded so fiercely the white handkerchief in her breast pocket quivered. Her throat went bone dry and all but swelled shut with a huge constricting knot. Ten feet behind the table where Dugan sat dead center, she could feel the intense energy radiating from him. The energy that was uniquely his, whether he sat atop an Appaloosa, or in his pickup, or at the dinner table boring into her with simmering brown eyes that had told her dessert would be in the bedroom.

From her seat at the end of the table, Lila shot her niece a commanding look that told Claire to get a grip. Otherwise she'd blow forever any chances she had of landing the directorship. Hands trembling, Claire retrieved the folders from the floor. With a steadying breath, she pulled from deep within the strength that had enabled her to survive that first lonely year in Philadelphia.

Damn Dugan! He'd driven her from town once. She wouldn't let him do it again. She would just have to ignore him and do one hell of a job convincing everybody else how much Sierra needed her.

Easier said than done, she thought, taking another deep breath.

She worked her way down the table, handing each board member a portfolio, shaking hands and smiling. When she reached Dugan, she thought her knees would buckle. Claire held her breath while his fingers lightly brushed hers and sent her reeling. She hoped he could read the pleading in her eyes. *Please, give me a break. Just treat me like a stranger.* But he flashed his dimpled smile and said in that husky voice that had whispered scorching endearments in her ear, "Welcome back, Claire."

"Thank you, Dugan," she managed in a tiny voice. She moved on then, down the table and into the hot seat facing the board.

She waited an eternity while they flipped through her files. She knew without a doubt they had to be impressed with the time and thought she'd assigned to the task. After all, she'd grown up in Sierra. She knew the nature of the residents intimately, how much they prided themselves on their traditional values. She understood their frustrations at seeing the young people abandon the farming life of their elders. At watching them flee Sierra for fulfillment in the cities because the federal government paid them not to plant crops so prices wouldn't tumble. She knew what Sierra's residents needed. What programs, beyond the day-to-day running of the clinic, she could institute to improve the quality of life and bolster the pride of the small community.

If she was so confident, why did the five or ten minutes that passed on her watch feel like hours? Why was she suddenly aware of her skirt inching up to reveal the turn of her knees?

Dugan, thank God, focused his attention on her portfolio. Still, as his long, tapered fingers moved over the sheets, her breasts swelled and felt heavy beneath her pale blue linen jacket. No matter how hard she tried to push it from her mind, she remembered the way Dugan used to excite her by brushing his fingertips across her nipples before teasing them to hard, begging peaks with his mouth.

How could she possibly survive the interview? Everything about him, every gesture he made prompted memories, and damn him, good memories, not the later, painfully sad ones.

Dugan cleared his throat. "Claire . . . Dr. Linwood, this is a most impressive presentation."

"Thank you," she managed in a halfway normal voice.

"Each of us'll ask you a question or two. Then, if you like, you'll have the opportunity for your own questions."

She didn't want to know anything from Dugan except why he was the one directing the interview. She shot her aunt a piercing look, but Lila quickly glanced away. Why hadn't she told Claire what to expect?

Orville Garrison, bless his hard-cash soul, was the first to ask a series of questions. By their negative nature Claire decided she didn't have a snowball's chance in hell of landing the directorship. She decided to hell with the board, to hell with Orville and Dugan. She would stage a performance they wouldn't soon forget. If they turned her down, they'd well talk about her professionalism later.

"What I want to know . . . what we all want to know, Claire . . . is why you've applied for the job?" Orville demanded. "You haven't been back in, what? Ten, eleven years?"

"Twelve," Claire responded with an upward tilt of her chin. "All my life I've dreamed of giving Sierra the doctor the town's always needed. As I was growing up, I watched my friends break legs and suffer high fevers. Their moms had to drive them forty miles to the nearest doctor. You know I lost my folks, my mother to viral pneumonia and my father to kidney failure. While they might have died anyway from their illnesses, there was no doctor to diagnose them early or to see they had the best medicine could offer."

She paused, hoping she could deliver her last telling statement without her voice breaking. "And surely you recall I wasn't immune to the need for a resident doctor."

"Ah, yes," an embarrassed Orville said, nodding his bald head. "The baby."

Dugan glanced over the edge of his report, his soft brown eyes suddenly flickering with the same pain that clutched Claire's insides. He cleared his throat. "Any more questions, Orville?"

"Just one. I apologize for stirring up bad memories, Claire, but I still have to know. Is it the money? Or do you really want to live back here with us small town folks?"

Claire straightened in her chair, drawing on the detachment she'd learned in medical school. "If I'm your choice, I won't renege on my contract. That's a promise. I'd be glad to live here . . ." she paused, focusing her attention on anyone but Dugan ". . . for the rest of my life."

Dugan looked directly at her. Claire refused to meet his gaze.

Orville closed his portfolio. "That's all I want to know."

"Harvey, you're next," Dugan noted, calling on the hardware store owner. The glance Dugan sent Claire carried a strong measure of respect. She appreciated that more than he could possibly know. His confidence strengthened her ability to field the rest of the interview in a more relaxed manner.

Once she'd answered the last question, she asked some of her own. "If you select me for the position, who will I report to?"

Nine pairs of eyes, Lila's included, abruptly dropped their focus from Claire's face to the table-top in front of them. Dugan cleared his throat again. "You'd report to me."

"You?" Claire blurted out, at the same time regretting she'd revealed her feelings in that one telling word.

"Yes, me. Since the doctor's not to be concerned with financial matters, only the patients themselves, it'll be my job to attend to the accounting."

Claire was determined not to let her emotions flare up again. "Would I have the freedom to hire or fire help? I'd need a nurse and a receptionist, at least."

"You could pick who suits you."

"And the clinic hours?"

"Would be up to you."

"Would you have any objections to that volunteer program for the high school kids I mentioned in my proposal? Or the mentorships I want to establish for a couple of bright students who want to become doctors?"

"Darned good ideas," he responded, and Aunt Lila winked in support.

"We'll need a pharmacy," Claire added, intentionally using *we,* instead of *you* in her statement.

"Granted. You'd provide me with a list of what you'd need, and I'd tend to the orders. We wouldn't want our director tied up in paperwork when she — or he," he quickly qualified, "— should be doctoring."

"You've answered all my questions, then," Claire

announced. *Except why did you make me leave? Why did you stop loving me? Do I have a ghost's chance of getting this position with you on the board?*

"We'll get back to you by morning," Dugan said, and all the members stood to shake hands with her.

Somehow Claire managed to touch Dugan's work-weathered hand one more time before she left the room. After closing the curtained door behind her, she collapsed against the lobby wall.

Her stomach was clenching in hard knots. She was certain she would faint if she didn't find a chair soon. Recognizing the signs of extreme stress in her own beleaguered body, she opened her eyes and found Fred leaning against the registration desk, quietly observing her.

"Fred, thank God you're here. Could you give me a hand?"

He pushed away from the desk and hobbled to her side. "Somethin' wrong?" He helped her into a chair at the far side of the lobby, away from prying ears.

"I'll say there's something wrong. Why didn't somebody tell me Dugan heads the clinic's governing board?"

" 'Spose 'cause you didn't ask."

"Oh, I asked, all right. Aunt Lila out and out ignored me."

"Wouldn't a thought Dugan bein' on that there board would flutter your lashes, bein' as how you up and left him and all."

Strength suddenly flowed through Claire's limbs

41

like molten steel. "For your information, I didn't up and leave him."

"But Orville said—"

"What he wanted everyone to hear. Orville's had it in for me since my father flunked his son in high school physics and kept John from playing football his senior year. Orville swore then he'd get even." Her vision blurred with the memories. "Daddy died before Orville could exact his pound of flesh, so he took out his revenge on me. Boy, did he ever! What did Dugan say after I was gone?"

"Nothin'. Just moped around mainly. Didn't smile for a month of Sundays. Claire, you broke that young man's heart."

"I broke *his* heart?" she flung back, hardly able to believe her ears. "Fred, I never thought you'd judge me like that. I don't feel like talking about it just yet, but someday I'll tell you exactly what happened. Suffice it to say, if anybody did any heart-breaking, it wasn't me."

The old man removed his straw hat and scratched his unruly mop of gray hair. " 'Spose if you'd givin' me the time of day, if you'd called, or maybe even scratched out your feelin's, maybe I would of understood what you're tryin' to say."

Claire's heart ached at the pitiful expression on Fred's lined face. Why hadn't she thought of the others she'd been forced to leave behind? Of the possible misunderstandings and confused loyalties? Why hadn't she realized Dugan wouldn't tell them the facts about her leaving?

"I'm sorry. Truly I am. I-I should have written. I

42

was hurting so bad, I guess I didn't realize you might be hurting, too. Will you forgive me, Fred?"

He pulled a wadded-up handkerchief from his pocket and wiped it beneath his bulbous nose. "You was like a daughter to me. I waited, and I waited. Every day I was sure you'd write." He stuffed the cloth back in the pocket of his gray work pants and shook his head. "Must've been powerful painful what happened to you, Claire. If only you'd told me . . ."

"Powerful painful is right, Fred." She reached up and gave him a tight hug around his neck.

At first he stood frozen in her embrace. Then slowly, as if the ice around his own heart was melting, he drew her close to his narrow chest. With his leathery hands, he patted her softly on the back as he used to do when she was a bereft teenager in desperate need of a comforting embrace.

"How'd it go in there?" he asked with a sniffle.

"Rough. I don't stand a chance."

"Now, now. Where's the sunshine?" he teased, lifting her chin and smiling into her watery eyes.

"Sunshine. Just what I need. Have you got an hour or so? I'd sure like to take a ride, and I don't want to go alone."

"I 'spose the hotel could spare me. Let me check with Miz Carter, and I'll meet you out front."

"Dugan's sure done well by himself," Claire said. She propped one foot on the tidy cross-railed gate of the barbed wire fence bordering Dugan's expanded

43

property. She marveled at the transformation in the gently rolling grasslands.

The one hundred and sixty acres no longer bore any resemblance to the rag-tag wheat and cotton farm she and Dugan had struggled to save from insects and drought. A new, ranch-style house, set back from the road a couple of hundred feet, sprawled across a verdant lawn. The red brick structure almost obscured the four-room frame farmhouse she and Dugan had shared.

To the west, eighty or so head of Black Angus cattle stood with backs to the wind, the hair gleaming on their sturdy bodies. To the south, summer wheat rippled in the gentle breeze, a sea of yellow against a cloudless June sky. To the east, cotton marched over the soil in meticulously contoured rows. Far in the distance Claire spotted what looked like an airplane hangar. Sand lined the borders of a long ribbon of black asphalt — a landing strip.

How could one man accomplish so much alone in a dozen years?

"Philadelphia suit you?" Fred asked, snapping off a weed he stuck between his teeth.

"It was okay. But I missed . . . this. I missed home," she quickly corrected herself.

"Guess you know folks're layin' bets you two young'uns'll take a crack at gettin' together again."

"Don't waste your money. Dugan didn't want me before. He won't want me now. Besides," Claire added, swallowing over the bitter resentment, "I couldn't think about starting up with him again."

"The little tyke you lost," Fred said. "Folks

44

say things was never the same for you after that."

Claire's gaze swerved to the family plot, where a miniature headstone marked Angela's grave. She was Angela's mother, and she hadn't even known the memorial had been erected.

"Folks don't have any idea what went on after Dugan and I lost . . . Angela." Even saying her name drove a stake of pain in Claire's heart.

She permitted her gaze to seek out the exact spot in the wheat field where she'd delivered Angela breech. Where the labor had begun hard and sudden. Without a phone and Ruby broken down, Dugan had run the mile to the next farmhouse for help. By the time he'd returned with Mrs. Flannigan, Angela had already arrived. Claire lay bleeding in the field, unconscious.

She shivered at the memory. Fred looped a consoling arm across her back. She took his hand in hers and smiled up at him weakly. "I never want anybody to go through what I went through. What Angela went through," she whispered. "That's one of the reasons I want to come back."

A rumbling sound in the distance caused Claire to glance up. Aunt Lila's 1967 Chevy was barreling down the winding, one-lane road from town. Lila pulled over to the side in a cloud of sand and dust.

She slammed the driver's door behind her and held up both hands as if she thought Claire might take a swing at her. "Before you start hollerin', I want to explain—"

"Why?" Claire demanded of her approaching

45

aunt. "Why didn't you tell me about Dugan. Why didn't you tell me he chaired the board!"

"Stupid question. If I'd told you, you'd have said no way in hell. You never would've agreed to fly down here and interview for the job."

"Well, I interviewed," Claire said, crossing her arms over her chest and expelling a sigh of disappointment. "I expect I know where it got me."

"And where might that be?" her feisty aunt wanted to know.

"On the next plane out of Texas. Good thing I didn't resign my position with the family clinic in Philadelphia."

Lila spread her fingers and frowned at a chip in her nail polish. "I wouldn't be makin' any hasty plane reservations, if I was you."

"I wouldn't think of leaving before we had a few days to catch up. And, to tell you the truth, I was hoping I could talk you into flying back east with me for a couple of weeks."

Lila rolled her eyes. "Will you just zip your lip and listen, sweet doctor niece of mine? I didn't drive all the way out here to be social. As it happens, I am on official business."

"What business?" Claire wanted to know, for a suspicious smile was beginning to play at her aunt's bright red lips.

"Dugan asked me to deliver a message. 'Course if he knew you was out here, he could of delivered it himself."

Claire gripped her aunt's forearms, a trickle of hope lifting her sagging spirits. "What is it?"

46

Aunt Lila shrugged coyly, clearly enjoying the drama of the moment. "He said . . ."

"Yes?"

"To tell you . . ."

"Aunt Lila!"

"That they've narrowed down the doctors they're considerin' to two."

"And?"

"You're one of them!"

Claire grabbed her diminutive aunt around the waist and lifted her off the ground. "All right!"

"Hey, now, you put me down."

"Who's the other doctor?"

"That good-lookin' weasel from Chicago." Lila harrumped loudly. "That guy's got a voice like Bing Crosby. Still, he can't hold a candle to you. But he's mesmerized a couple of the board members with his silky tongue."

"When do you vote?"

"Tomorrow morning."

Claire looked off in the distance, toward Sierra and a future she fervently hoped included her. "Oh, Aunt Lila. I don't think I can wait."

At Claire's request, Fred rode back into town with Lila. Claire wanted a few moments alone.

She wanted to stare out over Dugan's farm and face the memories the old house, the magnolia tree by the road they'd planted to celebrate their marriage, and the wheat field conjured up in her aching heart. Familiar organic scents assaulted her like a fist-swinging bully and propelled her back in time.

She closed her eyes to the smell of hay on the wind and recalled how she'd learned to drive the bucket of bolts Dugan called a tractor. Lacking the equipment to bail hay, they'd piled it in the barn — a quick glance told her the aging structure had been replaced by a newer version — then rolled around in it like playful children.

That night she'd picked hay out of their clothes, her body still singing from the romp that had evolved into a delicious afternoon of lovemaking.

A mournful howl penetrated her reverie. She opened her eyes and looked around. Could that possibly be Lazy Boy? The hound dog she and Dugan had found with a broken leg on the side of the road?

Instinctively she whistled what had been his summoning call. She heard a whimper and quickly scanned the landscape. There he was, lolling in the shade of the front porch. She whistled again, louder this time. Lazy Boy struggled to his feet and ambled arthritically across the broad expanse of grass where once only weeds had grown.

Claire dipped to her knees and reached through the fence to scratch Lazy Boy behind the ears. He whimpered and thumped his bony stick of a tail hard against the ground. Claire edged her face to the fence and was rewarded with a wet and welcoming lick.

"You want me back, don't you, boy?" As far as Claire could tell, that brought the sum of those glad she'd returned to four — Aunt Lila, Opal, Fred, and Lazy Boy, and she wasn't so sure about Opal.

But right now Claire wasn't thinking about the conspicuous absence of a welcoming committee. More than anything she wanted to pick a handful of wildflowers blooming by the fence, to climb over the gate's crossed wooden rails and place the bouquet on Angela's grave.

She hesitated. This was Dugan's farm. If she went on that property, she'd be trespassing.

Trespassing, hell! How could anyone deny a mother's need to pay respect to the grave of her only child? The only child she'd ever give birth to?

The bouquet Claire picked reflected the joy of the few short hours Angela had blessed her life. Claire reverently carried pinks and violets and cheerful daisylike blooms to the small cemetery.

The white wrought iron gate that bordered the family plot was unlocked. Three short steps brought her face to face with Angela's grave. Her headstone told the harsh reality of her life — Born and Died May 1, 1981. A chubby cherub in flight adorned the granite stone. Ironic, Claire thought, considering the thin little body that had been Angela's.

Claire bent over and touched the carpet of lush green grass before relinquishing her hold on the flowers. The grass, as dense as a putting green's and manicured as well, was velvet soft. Claire closed her eyes and remembered Angela's petal-fine skin, the tiny fingers she had balled into fists while she wailed and jerked her bony knees to her fragile chest.

Claire let her head loll back. The tears of a dozen years flowed freely from her heart. "Oh, Angela, I've missed you so," she murmured into the breeze.

Beside her Lazy Boy whimpered, as if he, too, still felt the devastation of the loss.

How long she sat like that, buffeted by the breeze and memories, Claire didn't know. She only realized she heard the gate's creak, felt Lazy Boy's tail thumping against her side, and a shadow blocking the warming rays of the sun from her face.

She glanced around and drew up short. "Dugan. I-I didn't hear you drive up."

Still in his suit, his tie flapping over his shoulder, he came to kneel beside her. "They told me I'd find you here." He plucked a piece of crabgrass from the turf over Angela's grave and stared down at it as he rolled the offending weed between his fingers.

The anger Claire thought she'd feel when she spoke with him again didn't materialize, only the sadness and the bond of loss. "Thanks for taking care of Angela. The headstone . . . the plot are . . . lovely."

"I tried to pick what I thought you'd want."

Now the anger came, for if he hadn't forced her to leave, he wouldn't have had to guess at what she'd wanted to commemorate Angela's short life. She could have helped Dugan choose Angela's headstone. They could have propped each other up, like normal parents grieving for a lost child. She could have planted flowers in a tidy row around the grave. He'd denied her all those opportunities that would have helped her cope with the oppressive burden of her grief.

Her hands, until now limp in her lap, balled into

50

fists. "If you hadn't made me go away, you would have known what I wanted."

"Claire, please. Not now. Not here." He squeezed her elbow in what he probably meant to be a consoling gesture, but it was more than she could bear. More than Aunt Lila's hug, more than Fred's tentative embrace, Dugan's simple touch triggered the flood of emotions she feared would swamp her when she returned to Sierra.

"I-I'd appreciate it if you wouldn't t-touch me," she told him in a quavering voice.

"I didn't mean anything by it. I . . . that is, you looked so unhappy sitting here, I thought you could use a . . . friend."

"A friend." The corners of her mouth dipped low. "A joke . . . considering."

"I'd like to be your friend."

"I'm not sure that's possible."

"Maybe in time," he allowed and rose to his feet. "Look, I'll just leave you alone," he added awkwardly. "Feel free to drop by anytime you like."

"Yes, I will. Thank you."

Claire stroked the soft turf over Angela's grave one last time, then stood before turning for her car. "You've done well for yourself, Dugan."

"I'd say we both have."

"How did you do it? How did you turn that dirt farm we struggled to save into . . ." she swept the landscape with her hand ". . . all this."

"Hard work. And I got lucky."

"How so?"

51

"Six months after you left, Orville called one night."

"What did *he* want?"

"His son — you remember John?"

"Oh, yes, I certainly do."

"John had just finished de-tox."

"De-tox? John? He's the last person I thought would ever try to dry out."

"He didn't have a choice. For a while Orville smoothed things over every time John got tanked up and plowed into somebody's mailbox. But one morning John broke into Marybell's Beauty Shop, drunk as a skunk. He trashed the place big time, then passed out in the shampoo bowl. Marybell pressed charges. John had two choices — de-tox or jail."

"That must have been hard for Orville to swallow."

"I imagine so. Anyway, John needed a place to stay for a while. Someplace where he wouldn't constantly wind up seeing that rotten bunch from on top he ran around with," he continued, referring to the towns west of Sierra, a thousand feet up on what was called the Caprock. "Orville asked if I'd let John work on the farm in return for room and board."

"So you did." Claire shook her head. "And in return, what did Orville do for you?"

"Nothing, for a while."

"Then?"

"John must have filled him in on the sad state of things around here. One day Joseph Witcomb

52

called to offer his prize Black Angus bull for stud so I could build my herd — no charge."

"And?"

"Orville helped in other ways."

"Like?" she asked suspiciously.

Dugan paused, as if hesitant to continue. "He loaned me some money."

"Wait a minute. You mean *after* I left, he loaned *you* the money we were desperate for? The money he refused to loan *us?*"

Dugan stared at his boots for a moment, then lifted an embarrassed gaze to Claire's face. "Yes, he did. I paid him off within a year."

She shook her head and silently cursed the unfairness of it all. "I don't want you to get the wrong idea. I don't begrudge you your success. But did it ever occur to you that Orville's help came at an interesting time? Considering the history of his threat to my father, didn't it ever cross your mind that Orville finally got what he wanted — revenge by hurting me?"

"Orville was no saint. I'll grant you that. But he's changed. And John helped me work the farm — "

"Like I never could."

"Claire, please. Can't we put all this behind us?"

"I can't forget, Dugan. I can't forget the weeks I cried myself to sleep in Aunt Sophie's boarding house. I can't forget the man I loved rejected me when I needed him most."

She glanced back at Angela's grave. Again Claire's heart shattered into a million pieces. A trembling seized her body. She crossed her arms over her chest, needing to finish what she had to say. "I can't believe you kept me from my little girl."

"I sent you away, but I didn't keep you from coming home."

"Oh no?" She swallowed the retort that would have put him in his place.

"Claire," he said, his voice now consoling, sympathetic. "Angela's gone. What's left of her is right here." He flattened his hand over his chest, and, with the other hand, placed a solitary finger to the corresponding spot on Claire's chest. "And right there."

At his touch all the nerve endings in Claire's aching chest sprang to life. She didn't want to feel the tingle of anticipation, the confusing urge to step into Dugan's arms at the same time she felt compelled to flee. "Don't touch me, Dugan. You have no right. Not anymore."

"I didn't mean that the way it may have seemed."

She smoothed her hands over her skirt and searched for an excuse to leave. "Look, I need to get back to town. I have a couple of phone calls to make."

"Has Lila told you the board's narrowed the choice down to you and that Chicago guy?"

Ah, a topic she could address without her voice quavering. "Yes, but after the grilling I went through, I figure there's no way I'll get the job."

"If that's true, how do you figure you convinced the board to vote for you over five others?"

"Just tell me one thing. Who's Orville supporting?"

"I'm not at liberty to say."

"You don't have to." Claire grinned wryly. "It's obvious he'll never get over what my father did to John. But I'm not sorry I applied for the job. If I hadn't — " she glanced back at the grave and bit her lip " — who knows how long it might have taken me to face coming to visit Angela."

And you, she added in the privacy of her heart. But she would never let Dugan know that. Despite the despicable thing he'd done to her, she couldn't stop loving him any more than she could cease breathing the fresh country air.

Dugan stood on his front lawn, watching Claire retreat to her car. He didn't move until the sedan disappeared down the road. He wished he could make her understand that sending her away had been the most difficult thing he'd ever done.

When she'd boarded that bus, her eyes had been dull and flat, as if she'd lost faith in the world, in herself. Now they were crystalline blue again, with a healthy, sometimes sassy spark. This evening they'd even glinted with anger and resentment. Away from him and the exhausting physical demands of the farm, Claire had recovered from her string of ailments.

Her bony frame had filled out to ripe curves and valleys. Now she even had breasts enough to fill his anxious hands.

He wanted to bury his face in her breasts, in her mass of unruly hair that kinked into the soft blond curls he'd always loved. Once again her hair shone with the luster of good health.

But something about Claire had changed, something that deeply troubled him. He'd hoped by going east, she might rediscover that bright-eyed trusting girl he'd fallen in love with. She was physically healthy and educated now, but he feared her unfailing trust and innocence had been the price. Instead there was a cynicism that saddened Dugan. She was a different woman.

He'd thought she might still bear some resentment toward him, but he was unprepared for the pricking nature of her words, for the none-too-subtle needling.

If only she knew the price he had paid, the sacrifice for her healing, the nights he had lain awake aching to hold her in his arms, to make love to her.

He knotted his hands into fists and fought off the familiar surge of physical need that rocked his body every time he fantasized about tucking her willing body beneath his.

He'd done his best to help her. Maybe his methods had been crude. Maybe he deserved her aloofness, but he damn well didn't deserve her abuse.

And Miss Claire Linwood — he winced at the fact she'd taken back her maiden name — had better patch up her attitude. Or she'd find herself in that Philadelphia family practice so fast her head would spin.

Chapter Three

In Claire's worst nightmares during her forced ex-
ile, she had returned to Sierra to find Dugan married to a devoted wife. One who'd gifted him with a
farmhouse full of brown-eyed, black-haired happy
children.

Claire had pictured the awkward introductions at
church or in Imogene's Cafe, before prying eyes and
tongues that wagged once she walked out the door.

She flopped onto her back with a frustrated sigh
and stared at the shadows playing across her hotel
room's high tin ceiling.

The one thing she hadn't imagined was Dugan
single all these years. She had no one to blame for
her ignorance but herself. Every time Lila had
brought up Dugan in long distance conversation,
Claire had told her she didn't even want to hear the
man's name.

She almost wished he were married. Free and un-
encumbered, he was a significantly greater threat to
her emotional well-being than if he'd been securely

tucked out of reach by inviolable vows.

How was she supposed to deal with the clamoring of her heart, the cavorting of her pulse when he touched her, like today by Angela's grave?

Pretend he didn't exist?

"Sure, Claire, sure," she muttered out loud.

She crawled out of bed and moved to the window to look out over moon-washed Main Street. The winds had died down, for the summer she hoped. Through a crack in the sixty-five-year-old structure she heard the eerie hoot of an owl.

How different from Philadelphia, where, if she had an ounce of sense, she'd practice medicine.

What Dugan had revealed that afternoon should have been enough to douse any residual feelings for him, except resentment. She couldn't believe he'd accepted help from Orville. If Orville had only given *them* the loan Dugan had begged for, they could have hired extra help. She wouldn't have been in the wheat field at the onset of hard labor. Dear, Lord, couldn't Dugan see, she might not have lost Angela?

Those thoughts were churning around in her befuddled brain the next morning while she and her competition sat on the Victorian settees in the parlor. They were being ever so civilized, sipping cups of coffee and awaiting the board's decision.

Suddenly the hotel's front door banged open. Fred stumbled in, propping up a bleary-eyed teenager who was doubled over, clutching her stomach.

"Good heavens, get that girl over here!" Claire said, waving Fred to the settee. "Who is she?"

58

"I don't rightly know. I found her sleepin' on the bench in front of the bank this mornin'. She said she was just fine, to leave her alone. Then I went out to walk for a spell, and I found her rollin' around in the alley, whimperin' and cryin'."

"Go up to my room and get my bag," Claire instructed. "The door's unlocked."

"I'm a doctor. I'd like to help you," she told the carrot-haired girl, who wore raggedy blue jeans and a gray sweatshirt big enough for Gunther Boone. "What's your name?"

"P-Pamela S-Sue."

"Now you just relax, Pamela Sue. Tell me what hurts. Is it your stomach?"

Fat tears spilled over the girl's lids and streamed down her freckled, dirt-streaked face. She nodded, then squeezed her eyes shut and clutched her stomach. Even though the girl carried too much weight for her frame, Claire couldn't help noticing the telltale swelling in her abdomen.

"She looks like a minor," the Chicago doctor murmured. "You'd better get permission to treat her."

"Permission? This girl's in pain. If I wait, she could be in serious trouble."

"Suit yourself," he said, taking a wing-back chair by the fireplace. "Just don't involve me. I, for one, have a clean slate on my malpractice insurance. That's why I don't carry a medical bag."

Nor did most of the medical residents Claire knew in Philadelphia, but that didn't stop her. "I can't believe they're considering hiring that iceberg

59

to run the clinic," she muttered through her teeth as Fred handed her the medical bag.

"And he seemed like such a nice fellow."

"It's obviously a cultivated appearance."

Claire checked the girl's vital signs, then gently probed her abdomen and confirmed her hunch. The poor girl couldn't have been more than sixteen years old, yet her stomach swelled with the gentle mound of childbearing.

With the damp cloth Fred fetched from the kitchen, Claire washed Pamela Sue's ashen face, then bent to whisper, "How far along are you, sweetheart?"

"I-I don't know what you mean."

"I'm a doctor. I'm not passing judgment. I need to know so I can help."

The girl lowered her moist, blond-red lashes and bit the inside of her mouth. "I'm not sure."

"How long since you've had a period?"

"Five months."

"Five months. Hmm. Have you seen a doctor?"

She shook her head briskly.

"Then I'd say it's about time. I have a room upstairs. If you'd like, you can rest on my bed while I examine you."

"I don't have any money. Well, two dollars."

"Don't worry about that. I just want to make sure you and your baby are okay. Where do you live, Pamela Sue?"

The girl clammed up as if Claire had asked her to reveal a state secret.

"I won't tell anyone unless you say it's all right.

The information will be confidential, just between you and me."

"Promise?"

Claire smiled. She'd been through this routine more times than she cared to count back in Philadelphia. So many girls, still children themselves, carrying so many unwanted babies, and she would have given her eye teeth to trade places with any one of them. "Promise."

"Albuquerque," she whispered behind her hand.

"My. That's a long way from here. How did you get to Sierra?"

Pamela Sue said nothing, only wiggled her thumb.

"No wonder you don't feel well. Are your parents there?"

"I don't have any."

Even though as a doctor Claire had been trained to distance herself emotionally from her patients' problems, she couldn't help feeling sorry for the frightened teenager. She was overweight by at least twenty pounds, possibly from starchy foods. Her hair was matted with dirt and bits of grass. She'd probably slept in a field along the way, and heaven knows how long since she'd had a decent meal.

"How long since you've eaten?"

The girl lifted her chin. Pride shone bright in her green eyes. "I don't need charity."

"You may not, but that baby does. How long since you've had anything to eat?"

"This morning."

"What did you eat?"

61

"Peaches."

"Green?" Claire asked suspiciously.

She nodded. "It's all I could find."

Claire heaved a deep sigh. "Well, that's a relief. Once you get rid of them, you should feel a lot better."

"I've already upchucked twice."

"Your stomach is probably spasming. I have something in my bag that should stop that. Do you feel like walking now?"

Pamela Sue nodded and sat up.

"Good." Claire summoned Fred, who'd been pacing at a respectable distance in the hotel lobby. She turned to the Chicago physician. "If the board reaches a decision, I'll be upstairs in my room. You'll tell them, won't you?"

"Of course," he answered, then dipped his head quickly behind the weekly newspaper.

"I guess it's time to vote," Dugan said, wishing he had another cup of coffee. "And if it's all right with you folks, we'll do this as a secret ballot."

"No need. I expect it's pretty clear who's voting for whom," Orville said with a knowing wink at Dugan.

"Be that as it may, I'd prefer this way," Dugan maintained.

Orville planted one elbow, then the other on the table's oilcloth covering. He nailed each of the other seven voting members with one of his infamous piercing stares. Lila returned the gaze, measure for

62

measure, then snapped up the pencil and paper to register her vote. For the past two hours she and Orville had been waging a verbal battle, for and against Claire.

Dugan hadn't wanted Orville on the board. As bank president, his opinion bore more than the normal weight. But Orville had been adamant and had twisted a few arms to make sure he landed the position. Dugan only hoped all voted their consciences. Something about that Chicago guy made Dugan's skin crawl.

One by one the board members passed their ballots to him. One by one he opened them and read the choices registered in an assortment of scrawls.

"Dr. Linwood, one vote." He glanced at Lila. She beamed.

"Dr. Linwood, another vote."

Orville shifted in his seat and smiled at the remaining ballots in Dugan's hands, as if he expected the others to support his man.

But Dugan was the one smiling when the vote was tallied. When he read the final count, Orville's confident smirk faded to a stormy scowl. "We have a tie, ladies and gentlemen. Four votes for Dr. Linwood. Four for Dr. Paisley."

"Better vote again," Orville insisted. "This time, we'd all better use our heads."

"I hardly think that comment's appropriate," Dugan said, instinctively springing to Claire's defense.

"You got a better way of settling it?" Orville demanded.

"According to the rules we set up, we vote twice.

If there's still a tie, as board chairman, I break it," Dugan reminded him.

Orville grinned. Dugan had the sinking feeling Orville expected paybacks. Well, if he did, he could soak his head in a bucket of rain water. Regardless of what Orville expected . . . what Claire expected of her former husband . . . if the vote came to him, he would vote his conscience. Period.

But what was that? he wondered. Until yesterday evening, he'd thought Claire perfect for the job. Lord knew she'd sacrificed enough for it. Her letters of recommendation raved about her dedication, skills and performance. Dr. Paisley's support documents painted only an adequate picture of him as a physician.

Then yesterday at Angela's grave, Dugan had realized how much bitterness Claire had bottled up inside. Doubt had been niggling at him ever since. In sending her away, had he destroyed the best part of her — the open, loving, caring woman who had sacrificed so much for him? The woman who, if he cast his ballot for her, would serve Sierra as its only doctor?

Beneath his suit coat, a dampness coated his armpits, but not from the heat. Overhead, the ceiling fans circulated the cooled air. The ballots piled up in front of him. He counted them again.

Another deadlock, a fact he promptly announced. The others stood to mill around while he struggled for what seemed like an eternity with his decision.

The doctor from Chicago might be competent,

but, if Dugan read him right, he had the hide of an armadillo. Claire, on the other hand, had the heart of a saint. At least she used to before he'd sent her packing.

Suddenly his choice was clear. He'd robbed Claire of her youth, their child, her ability to bear children. The least he could do was grant her the chance to achieve her dream.

He cleared his throat and stood. All conversation abruptly ceased. Dugan faced Orville Garrison squarely. "Dr. Linwood."

"Lord, the man just voted his hormones," Orville bellowed.

Dugan thought Lila was going to punch the banker right in the nose. Instead she shot him a go-to-hell look and crossed to shake Dugan's hand.

"I take it back. You aren't a poor excuse for a man."

"I'm not what?"

"Forget it," Lila quipped and gave him a big hug. "Just glad to see you finally got your head screwed on straight."

Dugan chuckled. "You want to tell her?"

"Nope. Gotta be you."

"But, Lila . . ."

"Look, you two are going to be workin' together from here on out. Best you bury your hatchets now, make your peace, start all over again."

Start all over again. Dugan liked the sound of that. But, if yesterday evening was any indication, Claire wouldn't take kindly to that idea.

"Where is she?" Dugan asked, his palms suddenly damp.

Fred stepped into the room. "If you're lookin' for Claire, she's upstairs in her room, doctorin'."

"Who's sick?" Lila asked.

"A poor young girl I found out in the alleyway."

"Someone from here?"

"Nope. A stranger."

"Maybe you'd better tell her then," Dugan suggested.

Lila waggled a finger in his face. "Dugan Nichols, this is your job, and you're going to do it."

"But it doesn't seem proper going upstairs to her room."

"Proper, smopper. She's doctorin'. It's not like you two'll be alone in her hotel room. Get up there and tell her. I can't wait to see her face!"

Pamela Sue was resting peacefully when Claire heard the light rapping on the door.

Claire's heart lurched. She sat there for a few seconds, hoping against hope the members of the board had overlooked their prejudices.

A knock sounded again. This time she bolted from her chair to answer it. Please, please, please, she prayed, let whoever's on the other side of that door have a smile plastered on her face.

Halfway expecting Lila, she didn't even try to hide her anticipation as she flung open the door. Her smile abruptly faded. Dugan stood there, filling the empty doorway with his work-hardened frame. He wore a suit and a tie. He wasn't smiling.

"Dugan."

His gaze skimmed over her, from head to toe, then reverted to her eyes. "Hi, Doc. How's your patient?"

"Resting."

"Can I speak with you for a moment?"

"Sure," Claire answered hesitantly, and a memory flashed through her mind. She and Dugan had spent their wedding night in his grandfather's ramshackle farmhouse. After they'd made love, Dugan had promised her someday, when finances improved, he'd reserve the best room at the hotel for Mr. and Mrs. Dugan Nichols. He'd carry her over the threshold as the mark of a new beginning. Claire was in that room now, and Dugan stood in the doorway. Of course, he'd probably forgotten those words, as he'd forgotten his wedding vows.

"Umm . . . why don't we step outside?" she suggested.

Claire closed the door behind her, painfully aware of the outdoorsy smell of him, the dried-on-the-line scent of his clothes. As she moved into the narrow hallway, the old boards creaked. Claire's shoulder brushed against Dugan's arm. She glanced up briefly and found him studying her. At the sheer nearness to him, her composure slipped a notch. Her words stuck on a tongue now thick in her mouth. "I-I, that is, I guess the board's reached a decision."

"Yes, we have."

His face was impassive. No dimple broke a grin. Claire's heart plummeted. "And you came to tell me the choice isn't me."

His eyes bored into her, yet there was a telltale twinkle in the warm brown. "I didn't say that, did I?"

"You mean . . . ?"

He reached for her hand, for a formal shake. Her knees turned to rubber. She flattened her hand against the wall behind her for support. She blinked her eyes to make sure she wasn't dreaming.

"I mean, congratulations are in order, Dr. Linwood."

"Oh, Dugan." Claire pressed a trembling hand over her lips. She wanted to freeze this moment in her memory, a picture to savor. She thought of her parents and how much they would have enjoyed sharing her triumph. The exhausting weight of twelve years of study and sacrifice lifted from her shoulders. Suddenly everything was worth the effort.

She wanted to welcome the messenger with a squeal and a hug. Never mind that person was Dugan, and he'd probably voted against her. Never mind that she'd achieved her success in spite of him, not because of him. Never mind that what she was feeling amounted to more than excitement and appreciation. She wanted to share this feeling with someone she loved. Dugan, damn him, was still that man.

To keep from making a fool of herself, Claire thrust her hands in her pockets and smiled up at

68

him, but the effort sent tears streaming down both cheeks. "I can't believe it."

He lifted an awkward fist to her cheek and hesitated before thumbing away the tears.

She wanted to grab his fist and kiss it, to leap into his arms with a triumphant holler. Instead, she let her eyes drift shut and simply trembled at the incredible need to return his touch. Finally she opened her eyes and murmured, "Thanks. I'm a bit overwhelmed by the news."

"The news. Yes. I . . . thought you would be." He glanced at his hand, still moist from her tears. Then he looked at her with an honest, open gaze.

Please, let this moment pass, she prayed. If Dugan didn't move away from her soon, Claire was afraid she'd make that fool out of herself. She knew he wanted no more than friendship. She was determined to maintain that space.

Smiling slyly now, he opened his jacket and pulled out a white envelope from the breast pocket. "I'm authorized to give you this."

As anxious as a child, she ripped it open. Inside was a contract and a check issued in her name and signed by Dugan on behalf of the governing board.

"Nine thousand dollars!"

"Minus taxes. I figured you'd count one deduction."

"But I haven't started work."

"We thought our doctor would need starting up money. That's your first month's salary, in advance."

"Oh, Dugan, I've never had so much money at

one time in all my life." She clutched the check to her breast and whirled around in a full circle. "I'm going to buy some new clothes and a car and a new couch for Aunt Sophie."

"Be careful you don't dig yourself into debt," he warned with a frown and an arched brow.

"Debt. Right. Of course not."

"Everyone's waiting for you downstairs. We're having a formal reception followed by a buffet lunch. The whole town's invited."

"But I can't leave my patient," Claire protested. "She's either an orphan or a runaway and scared half out of her mind."

"Lila can stay with her. You can run up to check on her every now and then."

"Yes, yes, I guess she can." Claire's aunt was a retired nurse and more than qualified to look after Pamela Sue. Claire took one last peek at the exhausted girl.

When she turned back around, Dugan's eyes were fixed somewhere below Claire's waist, on her hips, she thought. She suddenly became aware of the violet bikini panties she wore beneath a suit of the same color. Was the line showing, she wondered?

"Claire . . ."

"Yes?"

"I want you to know how happy I am for you."

"Thank you, Dugan."

"I also want you to know, I won't get in your way. Of course, I'll be the one to med-evac patients who need to go to the hospital. And I'll have to stick my nose in the books, that sort of thing. I'll try to make

70

myself scarce. It's bound to be awkward at first, us living in the same town again."

"The thought had occurred to me," she murmured, not admitting that concern had crossed her mind frequently since her arrival in Sierra.

"Can we try to put the memories behind us?" he asked.

Impossible, she thought but tempered her answer. "As I told you yesterday, I'm not sure I can do that. Too much has happened between us."

"The hurt then. Can we try to forget the hurt?"

She considered that for a while and decided the time had come, truly, to start over again. "If we can't forget, at least we can forgive, Dugan."

Ignoring where she was, what he had been to her, and all the tragedy she had experienced with this devastatingly handsome man standing mere inches away from her, she lifted a tentative hand to his cheek. His skin was warm beneath her fingers. By the look in his eyes, she knew he, too, was thinking all the times between them hadn't been bad.

"As I recall, you can be a very sensitive man. I'm going to need that quality from you to make this clinic the best it can be."

"Sensitive," he repeated. "Funny, I didn't think that's a word you'd use to describe me, after—"

"Someday we'll talk about all that, but now—"

"Now, here's to a new beginning."

She smiled and started to pull her hand away. But Dugan, darn him, covered it with his. His was a warm hand, one that had driven her to mindless passion. Despite her resolve to the contrary, she

71

wanted so desperately to tell him to bring her lonely body to life again. But that fantasy amounted to nothing more than self-destructive behavior she had to learn to control.

"I always said," he whispered, with a dimpled grin and a gentle squeeze, "that you were one hell of a lady. And now, you're finally going to be one hell of a doctor. Our doctor."

Chapter Four

"A bit early to be making your monthly deposit, isn't it?" Orville asked. He hitched his belt over his watermelon-size stomach and swaggered across the bank lobby to the teller's window.

"These checks were piling up," Dugan said, wishing for once Orville would mind his own business. "I figured no sense in letting them sit when they could be earning interest."

Orville angled his head and stared at the half dozen checks Dugan pushed across the polished walnut counter to the teller. "Hunters' fees — am I right?"

Dugan nodded. "For quail season." He made a fair amount by granting hunters' leases to the fallow land he'd snapped up at a bargain price a few years back.

"I figured you'd be drifting in long about now." Orville ambled over to the window. "Seeing as how our doctor's arrived and all."

"Oh, really? I hadn't noticed." Dugan hoped he wouldn't go to hell for lying. However, he'd be damned if he'd admit to Orville his blood was racing through his veins as if he were a quarter horse driven to run a mile at a hard gallop.

Not ten minutes after his foreman had brought the news back from town that Claire had checked into the hotel, Dugan had hopped into his truck and streaked down the dirt road toward Sierra. The four weeks since she'd left — twenty-eight Xs on his calendar — had dragged by. His foreman had told Dugan if his worsening mood didn't improve, he could find himself another man.

He had begun to think Claire would never return. Thankfully, she had called to tell him the Philadelphia clinic had let her out of her contract because of slack business and an increase in their malpractice insurance rates. If she hadn't, he would have gone nuts worrying that she'd changed her mind.

"Nice car she's bought."

"Expensive car," Dugan allowed, glancing through the window at the snappy blue Lincoln Continental parked in front of the hotel. Claire apparently had developed a taste for luxury items since he'd sent her away.

"Least she could of done is order through Moses."

"Yeah, you would have thought."

"Gunther was in this morning, complaining about the bunch of packages he had to deliver to her that arrived from back east. She's sure blowing a bundle of our money, and none of it here in town.

74

With her spending habits, lucky you two called it quits."

"Us calling it quits is none of your business, Orville," Dugan said with a leveling stare. He stuffed his savings passbook into his pocket and resolutely strode to the door. "I think I need some fresh air."

Orville was still staring at Dugan as he stomped up the three steps to the hotel. If Orville thought he was going to complicate Claire's life now that she'd snared the doctor's slot, he had another think coming. Dugan didn't exactly approve of the way she was spending her money — she'd obviously gone into debt for her fancy car — but she deserved that fresh start in Sierra, and he was going to make sure she got it.

He gripped the handle of the hotel's front door and heard voices caught up in what sounded an awful lot like an argument. One of the voices was Claire's.

He could hardly wait to see her. Still, he hesitated, not wanting to intrude on a private conversation. Instead he peered through the frilly lace that curtained the door, and his breath caught.

There she was, at the foot of the stairs. Even though her back was to him, he'd know her anywhere by that mane of curly hair that tumbled past her shoulders. The soft cloud of blond that used to drift down over her breasts when she sat astride him, her head flung back and her eyes glazed with passion.

The muscles in his forearms knotted up with the need to rip the door off its hinges. Good thing

75

Claire wasn't alone. If she were, he'd probably sweep her off her feet and plant one hell of a kiss on those sweet lips.

Gunther's gravelly voice drifted through the seams of the closed door. "What's the matter, Doc? Emma's Boutique not good enough for you?"

Dugan watched him dump a load of packages into Claire's arms.

"That's not it at all, Gunther. I needed new things. I didn't have time to shop, so I ordered out of a catalog."

"Appears to me you've got that big city nose of yours stuck high enough in the air for a bird to land on. Staying at the hotel when you could've bunked with your aunt."

"Not that it's any of your business, but there's no room for me at Lila's. She's taken in that sweet girl, Pamela Sue. I'm here because I don't have any other place to stay."

She could have stayed with me, Dugan thought, but he'd known better than to offer her his spare bedroom.

"And what about before, when you came back to talk to those board folks?"

"For your information, Dixie Hinkle was at Lila's, by invitation. My aunt thought she'd need help after her back surgery."

"I hear one room wasn't good enough for you. You had to rent two."

Claire's voice rose in agitation. "I've worked hard to get where I am, Gunther. The rooms here are awfully small. I figure I can afford the luxury of connecting rooms until I find something permanent."

Gunther had no right to stick his nose into Claire's business, but he had a point about the extravagance of two rooms. Still, Dugan had relinquished any say over her habits, spending or otherwise, when he'd sent her away. But he still cared for her and wanted to see her prosper. If she dug herself too deep in debt, she might be asking for a whole lot of trouble.

"Yeah, I suppose you can afford anything you want," Gunther went on, "now that Sierra's makin' you rich."

Protective hackles bristled on the back of Dugan's neck. He jerked open the door. Deep pink blotches colored Claire's cheeks, but neither she nor Gunther appeared to notice he was standing in the doorway.

"I'll earn every penny I'm paid here and then some," Claire shot back at Gunther.

"Shame you couldn't come back until folks here promised you'd get rich."

Dugan had had enough. He strode into the lobby and insinuated himself between Gunther and Claire. Whether she wanted his interference or not, she was going to get it. He couldn't stand there and let Gunther talk to her that way.

"Don't you have something to do besides hassle the doc here?" He turned to scoop her packages into his arms. First Gunther scowled at him, but his antagonism faded, and he doubled over in a coughing fit.

"Hi, Doc. Welcome back. Where do you want these?"

"Upstairs, in my room." She pulled the key from her pocket and slid it into his shirt pocket, mouthing the words "thank you" and rolling her eyes.

Dugan's gaze snagged on the pout the word "you" created on Claire's lips. For two cents he would have grabbed her right then and there and met that pout with his hungry lips.

Fortunately, he didn't have two cents on him. Trying to act nonchalant and merely friendly, he winked at her and turned to deliver her packages to her room.

"I want you to come see me, Gunther," he heard Claire say. "That cough of yours is getting worse."

"I told you before. I don't need no doctor."

"You come see me anyway. The clinic should open in a week, if the interviews go as planned this morning. In the meantime, try to cut back on the smoking, will you?"

"In a pig's eye!"

Hearing Gunther's boots grind into the floor, Dugan figured the confrontation was over. At the top of the stairs he glanced back and caught Gunther glaring at Claire with unmistaken malice. He waited, deciding she might need him again.

"Say, Doc?" Gunther said.

"Yes?" she answered wearily.

"Don't you go hurtin' that man again. When you up and left him for the big city, it about kilt him."

* * *

By the time Dugan returned with Claire's key, she was fit to be tied. She tried not to let her anger at Gunther's unjustified accusation spill over on Dugan. She wanted to live in peace with him. She didn't want to resurrect the pain and sadness any more than he did.

But how could she keep the promise she'd shakingly made Dugan in the hotel's hallway four weeks ago when people like Gunther carried irrational grudges against her? When they blamed her for something Dugan had done?

"Gunther got to you, huh?" he said, as they crossed the street on their way to the clinic.

Claire expelled a deeply drawn sigh. "I don't understand what it is that man has against me."

"You're successful. He barely ekes out a living."

"You're doing well. He doesn't treat you like you have your hand in everybody's pocket around here."

"He probably resents the fact you left Sierra for the big city."

"Which is whose fault?"

"Claire . . ."

"All right, all right. I did promise."

"Give him time. I'm sure he'll come around."

"He'd better come around—to see me, that is. That cough sounds terrible."

"Tell you what. I'll hogtie him, and you can give him the once over."

"Like we used to do when we rounded up those scraggly calves," she said, with a hearty laugh.

Dugan's eyebrow shot up. His voice dropped a full octave. "I didn't think you remembered."

"Well, I . . . that is, of course I remember." How had she let the memory slip, and in front of him! She patted her stomach. "I still have a scar to show for it."

"Ah, yes, the scar." His gaze slid suggestively over the fullness of her breasts to her lower abdomen. "I do seem to remember."

A hot flush crept over Claire's cheeks. The calf had ripped the tender flesh on her stomach with the flailing kick of a hoof before Dugan could tie him up. For days Dugan had cleansed the wound for her and smoothed salve on the angry tissue. A couple of times his fingers had strayed . . .

Trying to wipe such thoughts from her mind, she walked beside Dugan in awkward silence. It was three blocks to the clinic. When they passed Imogene's Cafe, Opal waved. They returned her greeting in kind.

Ironic. How many times had she and Dugan strolled past that cafe as husband and wife, their hungry eyes yearning for a piece of pie they couldn't afford? Now they had the financial resources to buy the cafe, lock, stock, and barrel. But they'd lost something far more precious than money along the way.

At the corner of the bank, they took a sharp right. Two blocks down the side street, past three frame houses and a baseball field, stood the spanking new Sierra Medical Clinic. Including the graveled parking lot to the right, the clinic occupied most of half an acre.

Claire paused across the street and admired the

one-story stucco building that gleamed white in the hot July sun. The thought that she would own half this building in five years sent chills of pleasant anticipation skittering over her arms.

"You like it?" Dugan asked.

"I love it! Especially the trees. I'm glad you caught the builder before he bulldozed them."

A light breeze shook the branches of two majestic oaks, the sound not unlike a gentle, spring rain. Beneath the trees posted on either side of the clinic like sentries, a profusion of fragrant pink petunias danced in freshly tended beds.

Petunias. Claire smiled at memories the ruffly blooms evoked. When she first moved to the farm, she planted petunias beneath their bedroom window. The heady sweet nectar had wafted through the window at night.

Dugan gestured at the half-full parking lot. "I hear you've got a dozen folks lined up to interview."

"Some nurses, I hope."

"Two, I think."

"Good. If they're qualified, I'll probably hire them both and rotate their hours."

"Got any ideas who you want for receptionist?"

"As a matter of fact, I do."

"Who would that be?"

"You remember the sweet girl I treated that day in the hotel?"

Dugan frowned. "The pregnant one?"

Something inside Claire bristled at Dugan's point of reference. He could have referred to Pamela Sue as the girl with the carrot-red hair. Instead he chose to focus on the fact she was pregnant. "Her name's Pamela Sue, and she could use the job."

"Lila's put her up in her spare bedroom. She's working off the rent by cooking and cleaning."

"She still needs a job, for self-respect, as much as anything else. From what Aunt Lila tells me, she's had a rough life. And she'll need money when the baby comes. I'll deliver it no charge, of course, and her bill will be covered at the hospital. But she'll need diapers and formula and—"

"Since Sierra's supporting that clinic, don't you think that job should go to someone who lives here?"

"She does live here," Claire maintained.

"Who knows how long?"

"Look, Dugan, no offense, but I think the job should go to the person who needs it the most."

"In your opinion."

Claire studied the hard set to Dugan's chin and decided he was serious. "But you won't make the decision."

"Now, Claire . . ."

"Don't 'Now Claire' me. I asked you point blank during my interview who would have the authority to hire. You said I would."

"Yes, but—"

"I won't budge on this, Dugan."

"Hiring an out-of-towner won't be a popular decision around here. Lots of ladies would love to have a part-time position that doesn't require a lot of skill."

"I expect I'll make lots of decisions that won't be

82

popular." Claire lifted her chin and marched across the street. Dugan followed. "But as long as I do the job I was hired to do, no one has a right to criticize me for whom I employ, and that," she added, shooting him a determined look, "includes you, Dugan Nichols."

Dugan said nothing, only compressed his full lips into a hard slash of a line and stared straight ahead. She remembered that look only too well. The last time she'd seen it had been the day he'd awakened her with the news she was leaving on the next bus out of Sierra.

He could scowl all he wanted. Claire was no longer the pitiful, frail creature he'd ramrodded into leaving. She would make the decisions concerning the clinic's day-to-day operations, with or without Dugan's blessing.

"I was merely expressing an opinion, Doc."

"I don't need your opinion."

"Tell you what then." He narrowed his gaze and shoved his straw hat onto the back of his head. "I won't give it to you. Matter of fact, I'll make myself scarce around here."

And before she could think of something as stingingly sarcastic to fling back at him, he spun around and strode off, digging a hole in the emerald green turf where his heel had been.

"Fine with me," she murmured at his broad, retreating back. But she knew before he'd reached the corner, that that was a colossal lie.

* * *

Claire hired Pamela Sue anyway. The girl's eyes glistened with tears when Claire delivered the news she could work mornings until school started, then afternoons until the baby came.

Claire figured that by working with Pamela Sue, she might be able to coax the teenager to tell her more about her family and the baby's father. Then, maybe Claire could really help her — and the child that would bless her tragic life in three short months.

Although Claire had prepared herself to defend Pamela Sue's presence in the clinic, she needn't have bothered. True to his word, Dugan remained at arm's length.

On Monday mornings she would arrive to find he'd audited the bookkeeper's records over the weekend. He'd scribble any message he had for her on a scrap of paper. Claire tried to tell herself that she wanted to be left completely alone by him so she could concentrate on doctoring.

Occasionally she ran into him at lunch at Imogene's, and the lonely part of her deep inside sparked to life. She was sorely tempted to pull him into her booth under the guise of talking clinic business.

But the moment they were both in the cramped cafe, all conversation halted, as if everything between them was the whole town's business. Claire got the distinct impression if she looked at Dugan the wrong way, someone would instantly spring to his defense. The tension was so thick, Imogene could have sliced it and served it for lunch. So slowly Claire and Dugan would tear their gaze from one another, and she would lose her appetite. She finally resorted to eating lunch in her office.

She loved her work. One by one the townsfolk sought her out for physical exams. There were the usual cases of influenza, strep throat, athlete's foot, and ear infection. In between appointments, she held a class on infant care for Pamela and three other pregnant women.

Her biggest thrill was discovering a tumor the size of a fist in the lung of a local farmer. She scrambled to assemble a team of specialists in Lubbock, who ran the patient through a battery of tests and decided he was a candidate for surgery.

When the phone call came from the surgeon that the tumor had been encapsulated, and the cancer hadn't spread, she threw a party at the clinic to celebrate. She even invited Dugan. This was what a doctor lived for—to make a difference, to save lives.

She could tell that the resentment most of the townsfolk felt toward her was slowly but surely disappearing. Day by day the barriers fell away. The feeling of belonging was comforting, yet the hole of loneliness inside her grew bigger every day. She didn't want to admit that only Dugan could mend the hurt, but the truth was, only he could.

Exactly one month after the clinic's grand opening, all hell broke loose at about five o'clock. Upon raising a window to air out a first-story room, the hotel's maid had been stung by a dozen wasps. As Claire was about to give her an antihistamine injection, a child's anxious wail echoed through the clinic. Claire's nurse swept in and ordered her into the next room. There an hysterical mother sat holding her equally hysterical two-year-old son who had suffered a nasty compound fracture to his right arm.

By the time Claire had pacified and treated both patients, all she wanted was a quiet meal and amiable conversation. Lila had driven Pamela Sue into Lubbock for an ultrasound examination and hadn't returned. The nurse and bookkeeper had made dinner plans with their families. The prospect of eating alone at the hotel was enough to squelch Claire's hunger.

She gazed out her office window and sighed.

A teenage boy and girl strolled along the quiet street, arm in arm. Their faces shone with the radiance of health — and young love.

Claire sighed. In the carefree days before her parents died, she and Dugan used to take walks like that. Her mother invited Dugan over for supper every Sunday. Afterward, they studied and tried to ignore the call of passion. When the desire to touch become too great, they excused themselves for a walk . . . and a bit of privacy.

And she was intruding on this couple's privacy, she thought with a pang of conscience. She turned from the window to pencil her comments on her last two patients' records.

The screech of tires followed by a loud metallic crash disrupted the peaceful evening. The floor beneath her shook. The air crackled with violent energy.

"What in the world?" Claire wheeled around and pushed the blinds aside.

Her first thought was that some drunken driver had careened down the street, and that the innocent couple could be in trouble.

She looked out the window and her heart plunged to her feet.

Chapter Five

"Dugan!"

Outside the clinic, at the parking lot entrance, Dugan's shiny new pickup had rammed head-on into the trunk of the sturdy oak tree. Smoke billowed up from the truck's crunched engine. Through the haze, Claire saw Dugan slumped over the steering wheel, his body still, unmoving.

For a moment she couldn't budge from the window. She was the woman who'd been married to Dugan, the woman whose fierce love for the Texas farmboy had never died.

Then the physician in Claire seized control of her shaken body and her resolve. She grabbed her medical bag and bolted for the door.

Please don't let his injuries be serious. Please give me the strength to help him, she prayed, unable to quiet the fear that clutched her heart.

As she tore out the building and raced to the pickup, she reminded herself of her months' duty in that emergency room in Philadelphia.

She was a doctor. She was trained. She could

treat whatever injuries Dugan had sustained.

She reached the cab at the same time as the teenagers she'd seen strolling outside the clinic. The boy grabbed the cab's door and gave it a powerful yank. It opened with a loud, cracking pop. Claire took one look and grabbed the door for support.

Blood. Dugan's blood. All over him. All over his truck. The familiar and sickeningly sweet smell of it blended with the acrid smoke that coated Claire's nostrils.

Hazily Dugan lifted his head and regarded her with a bleary gaze. "Doc . . . do you think . . ."

"He's alive!" the girl shrieked, echoing the relief that shot through Claire's aching chest.

"Dugan," Claire said, reaching out to check his pulse, "I'm just going to—"

But before she could say another word, he tumbled from the truck's cab into a crumpled heap at her feet.

Claire knelt to Dugan's side and pressed her fingers to his neck. A weak pulse fluttered beneath her trembling fingertips. He wouldn't live long if she didn't move him and move him fast. He'd lost far too much blood.

As if to warn Claire, steam spewed from the engine in a menacing hiss.

"We've got to get him out of here," she ordered the boy and his date. "The truck could explode any minute."

"I'll get his shoulders. You grab his feet," the boy told the girl. "Geez, will you look at that leg!"

Blood pumped from the inside of Dugan's upper thigh and coated his ripped jeans in a sticky burgundy ooze. Claire suspected he had either punctured or severed his femoral artery. She prayed for only a puncture, an injury serious enough in itself. If he'd severed the artery . . . She didn't want to think about Dugan's chances if his injuries were that serious.

"Quick. Get him inside the clinic. First room on the right. Try to keep him level. I think it's his femoral artery."

"Is that bad?" the girl asked.

"It's bad all right. If we don't get a compress on that artery soon, he could bleed to death."

Claire moved with efficiency, snapping orders, thinking fast. She hated to lose a patient, any patient, but she couldn't, she wouldn't let Dugan die, damn him. No matter how much he'd hurt her, she still cared for him. Cared for him a whole lot more than she'd realized until that moment.

She had things to say to him, whether he wanted to hear them or not.

The boy—Adam—followed her orders with deft hands and a clear head. He served as her assistant. His girlfriend, Becky, helped, too. However, from the ashen look on Becky's face, Claire feared that she might faint any minute. The nauseating smell of the blood and the sheer volume of it splattered around the treatment room might overwhelm her.

"Are you with me?" Claire asked the girl.

She nodded vaguely.

"Good. I want you to call for help. A nurse. Two numbers on my desk telephone. Two doors to the right."

Becky nodded and disappeared down the hall.

"Adam, in the cabinet up there, sterile gauze bandages. Get all you find. Open a box. Yes. Now, give the bandages to me."

Claire pressed a thickness of gauze to the gushing wound in Dugan's leg.

"Get a blanket. Quick! The cabinet to your right. He's going into shock. Yes, yes, that's good. Now, here." She grabbed his hand and thrust it atop the gauze at the crease of Dugan's crotch. "Keep up the pressure on the compress. I've got to cut away his jeans."

Dugan moaned, apparently conscious. Good. He grabbed for his leg.

"Oh, no, you don't. Be tough, Dugan. I've got to cut away your jeans. It's not going to feel good."

As she worked, Dugan thrashed his head from side to side, uttering a string of scorching expletives she'd never heard pass his lips. But then she guessed there was a lot about the man she'd never known.

The jeans were snugger than Claire had thought from her days of silent admiration. She slipped the surgical scissors into a tear in the shredded denim and forced her fingers to clip one leg from the bloodied jeans. Beneath the fabric, she found several diagonal cuts slashed across his upper thigh, in addition to the artery injury.

"Lord, what'd he do to his leg?" Adam asked.

"It's anybody's guess," Claire muttered. "But look at his boots."

"Yuck. Cow dung."

"So he was probably in the pasture. Infection could be a problem. When we finish patching him up, I'd like your help cutting off those boots."

"He isn't going to like losing them."

"He's got others," Claire told him. "Besides, pulling them off would cause too much trauma to his wounds. He's lost so much blood as it is. I can't risk him losing more."

"He is going to make it, isn't he?" the boy asked, as if he needed her assurance.

"He's got to make it," Claire answered, as much to Dugan as to the boy. "He's got some nasty wounds I need to cleanse. Until the nurse gets here, I'll have to depend on you to help me. Can you do it?"

"Just tell me what to do."

"Keep pressure on that artery." She bent her ear to Dugan's chest and listened. His heart thumped erratically.

She reached behind her and grabbed two bottles of hydrogen peroxide from a small refrigerator. She unscrewed the lid to one. "How's your girlfriend?"

"Managing."

"Could she help?"

"Becky!" he called over his shoulder.

The girl moved shakily into the doorway, her fingers pressed tight against her lips. "The nurses weren't home. What are we going to do?"

"Make do. Quick, take Adam's place."

The girl swallowed hard and obeyed.

"Apply pressure on that bandage. Yes, that's good. That's great, Becky.

"Now, Adam, you grab Dugan's arms. When I pour this hydrogen peroxide on him, it's going to hurt like hell. Don't let him thrash. I can't have him falling off the table. Ready?"

"Ready."

She poured the cool liquid onto Dugan's wounds. Dugan lurched. He gritted his teeth and pulled against the boy's hold on his arms. Still Claire poured, watching the liquid bubble over the raw, oozing flesh.

"Wasn't he your husband?" Becky asked.

Claire nodded, but she didn't meet the girl's imploring gaze.

And he still would be my husband, if he hadn't been in such a hurry to get rid of me.

If Claire had wrestled a bull, her body couldn't have ached more. Eighteen hours had dragged by since she'd arranged to have Dugan's litter moved to one of the beds in her hotel suite. She had been assisted by concerned citizens drawn to the clinic by the commotion.

She didn't care what the town busybodies said. In her suite Dugan would be more comfortable than on the clinic's narrow treatment table. Installing him here also meant that she could maintain a comfortable vigil at his bedside for the critical first twenty-four hours. She wanted to be the one to abrade the oozing flesh on his thigh every four hours. She wanted to be near him when he regained consciousness.

The fact she hadn't slept a wink or eaten wasn't the reason fatigue racked her body. As an intern and a resident, she had adjusted to long hours and intense demands. She'd treated patients with more life-threatening injuries than Dugan's and felt better than she did now.

After she'd shooed the volunteers from her room, her professional facade had crumbled. Her emotions had seized her in alternate waves of shakes and tears. If Dugan hadn't found her in time, he could have died from his wounds.

She watched him sleeping fitfully in her bed and shuddered at the thought of never seeing or touching him again.

The door creaked open. Lila stuck her head into the room. She'd returned from Lubbock in time to assist with the final clean-up at the clinic. "One more hour, and it's sleep for you, young lady."

"I'm not a young lady, and I'm not tired."

"And toads don't hop. One hour."

Claire waved her aunt from the room and sank into the rocker she'd pulled to Dugan's bedside. She'd just lean back and close her eyes until he surfaced.

No sooner had she closed her eyes than Dugan stirred in his semiconscious state. Claire sat up with a start. She found him pulling against the terry cloth towels that bound his wrists to the frame of the single bed.

"Dugan?" she called. "Dugan?"

He didn't answer. He only relaxed into the softness of his pillow.

Just as well, Claire thought from a doctor's perspective. She readjusted the sandbags securing the pressure bandage over his punctured artery. If she could keep him still eight more hours, his artery might heal without surgery.

She checked the flow rate on Dugan's IV and prayed the broad-spectrum antibiotic she'd prescribed would ward off infection. God only knows what bacteria had contaminated his wounds.

His head lolled to the side. His eyes fluttered half open. He licked his lips and muttered weakly, "Claire . . . Claire."

He'd called her Claire, not Doc. Hope welled up inside her. Except during the interview, he'd rarely referred to her by Claire since her return to Sierra. It was as if he wanted to show her that's all she was to him, the town doctor. Now that he was in pain, had he let his guard down?

She curled her hand over his forearm and squeezed gently, then slid one fingernail into the swirl of black hair tinged reddish-gold by the summer sun. "I'm here, Dugan," she assured him.

"Oh . . . there . . . you . . . are. Bed."

"Yes, you're in bed." She chuckled at the irony. "My bed. We moved you here to my hotel suite, where you'd be more comfortable."

His eyes drifted shut again. Deep vertical lines

furrowed his forehead. "Never . . . could . . . take . . . you here."

The fact he remembered they'd talked about a delayed honeymoon in the hotel shook Claire, but she tried not to make too much of the reverie. Patients' thoughts often wandered to the past when they were in pain.

Claire squeezed his arm again. Before she administered another injection of pain killer, she wanted him to talk more, if possible. She needed to know more details of the accident in order to treat him properly. She also needed the assurance his condition was improving.

"Dugan? Dugan?"

His eyelids fluttered. "Hmm?"

"Can I get you anything? A sip of water? A chip of ice?"

"No. No." He paused, then added, "Let . . . go."

Let go? He wanted her to let go of his arm? Stinging from the request Dugan had mumbled, even in the clutch of pain, she reluctantly released his hand. If she'd ever entertained fantasies that he had regretted ending their marriage, his words just now doused any hope she had harbored.

"Skin . . ."

"Hurts, I'll bet. Yes, well, I'll give you another shot soon."

"Hurt . . . Claire. Don't want to . . . hurt . . . Claire."

"I'll do my best, but I can't make all the pain go away," she told him, even as she thought that was a strange thing for Dugan to say. Unless his body had changed over the years, he was one of those rare people blessed with a high threshold for pain.

"Skin . . . ny."

"Skinny? You're anything but skinny." She let her admiring gaze slide over his body. His muscles were even better defined than when she'd caressed him years ago with willing hands.

"Bones. Skin . . . and . . . bones," he murmured. "Claire."

He was talking about her then? And he thought she was skin and bones?

Claire glanced down, over her full breasts to what she considered healthy thighs. If Dugan thought she was skin and bones, he was either near-sighted or truly delirious. At five and a half feet, she now carried one hundred and thirty pounds on her frame. Hardly what she'd call skinny.

"Gonna . . . die."

"You aren't going to die, Dugan." She smoothed an errant lock of dark, wavy hair from his forehead and patted his cheek with an open palm. "Not if you listen to what I say. You'll have to—"

"If . . . I . . . don't . . . send her . . . away."

Claire's hand froze on Dugan's cheek. Send whom away? Her again? Someone else? What in the world was he talking about?

Before she could make sense of his barely coherent thoughts, he turned his hand over, palm up. "Take . . . this."

"What is it, Dugan?" She moved her hand to his. She did this partly because she didn't want him to pull free from the cloth restraints, partly because something inside her compelled her to. "What is it you're handing me?"

"Ticket. Bus. So . . . phie." Eyes closed, he winced and moaned.

The pain might as well have been shooting through Claire's body. She darted to the makeshift medication table she'd assembled in the corner. Dugan's strange words tumbled around in her head.

Where, in his pain and drugged mind was he? And more specifically, in what time was he?

Now?

She didn't think so. He'd mentioned a bus ticket and Sophie. That could mean only one time — twelve years ago, when he'd sent her away.

She measured the precise dosage of medication into the syringe and returned to Dugan's side. She lifted his sheet, deftly inserted the needle in his rock-hard hip, then drew the sheet back over his broad chest.

The moment she touched his chest, something tugged on her whole being. How she wanted to give in to the pull. For how many nights had she dreamed about snuggling up to Dugan again? For how long had she imagined resting her cheek on his furry chest and listening to his heart beat beneath her ear?

Here was her chance, finally. Her last chance to touch the man who had been her husband. It would be worth it, even if he couldn't meet her lips, or remember the feel of them.

She bent over his chest, careful not to brush against him. Then, she closed her eyes and softly, oh so gently, pressed her lips to his stubbled cheek.

And tasted salt.

Salt? From what? Tears?

Her eyes snapped open. She looked closely to confirm her suspicion. She touched his cheek with the tip of one finger. Moist. No, wet. Tears. She'd tasted tears.

Shed for what? Pain?

Suddenly the string of words he'd uttered fitted together in her mind, pieces of a verbal puzzle.

Let go, Claire. Don't want to hurt Claire. Skin and bones. Claire. Gonna die . . . if I don't send her away. Take this ticket. Bus. Sophie.

"Oh, Dugan, what are you trying to tell me?" Claire cried. "Is it possible—that is, did you. . . ? Dear Lord, did you send me away because you were afraid if you didn't I'd die?"

The shuffling of feet, the mumbling of voices. Cool air on his bare legs. Ice cold liquid on his thigh.

That turned to fire! Where was he, and why the hell was someone torturing him?

Gripping fistful of something padded in his hands, he pushed against his eyelids and squinted into a blurry, gauzelike light.

Wherever he was, the place smelled antiseptic, except for a hint of . . . yes . . . Claire. He'd remember her scent anywhere. Clean. Floral. Sweet, so sweet. "Claire?"

"Thanks for the compliment, Dugan-boy, but I'm no Claire."

That voice . . . Lila's. Claire wasn't there after all. He must have been dreaming again as he had for so many lonely nights. Dugan sank back into his pillow, fighting the pull of sleep.

"I just kicked Claire out of here. Poor girl's been watching over you twenty hours straight. Hold still now. Seein' as how you've come around, you're going to feel this a sight more."

The heat in his thigh flamed to fire. He scorched the walls with every word a man shouldn't use in the company of a woman. Back when he was a strapping boy of seven, before his mother ran off with his father, she used to scare him into finishing every last one of his chores. She told him if he didn't, someday the devil would drag him into the depths of hell.

Dugan figured he must not have finished a few chores, because his body burned with hell's fury.

Especially down there, near his groin. What the hell was Lila doing anyway? Jesus—here came the fire again! He stiffened his body and gritted his teeth. "What are you doing?" he bellowed, suddenly awake, coherent. "Torturing me?"

"Nah. Just testin' to make sure you're conscious."

"Hell, yes, I am. Are you satisfied?"

"My, aren't we gettin' testy."

"Where's Claire?"

"Soon as I finish dressin' your wounds, I'll fetch her. Don't you go keepin' her too long, though—you hear?"

Dugan heard a door open, close and that blessed, lyrical voice. "Did someone call me?"

Dugan forced his eyes fully open. Claire glided across the room, a blur of blond and blue and white. He dug his elbows into the mattress and tried to sit up. "What's up, Doc?"

Lila's hand shot out and shoved him back into the bed. "Not you! You're not goin' anywhere, up or down. Least not for a week. Right, Claire?"

"Right." Claire moved to Dugan's side and granted him a glorious smile. Before he could reach over and touch her to make sure she was real, Lila drew her aside to talk in hushed whispers.

In his befuddled state, Dugan decided if Claire would stand there smiling at him, he'd hang around—wherever he was—for a week. Shoot, maybe longer.

He cast his gaze around the room and frowned. He was in . . . a hotel room. Hmm.

He steered his focus across the room. He couldn't be sure, but he thought Claire's parents stared back at him. They'd been dead since she and Dugan were high school seniors, so that would be a picture, then. He squinted again. Yes, he saw a frame.

So he was in Claire's room?

"You're in my room," he heard her say, and he focused his bleary gaze bedside. "Do you know why?"

He wasn't in so much pain he couldn't think of a good reason why he'd crawl into Claire's bed. But instinct told him something more than hormones had delivered him to her room.

Suddenly scenes in his far pasture flashed before his eyes. Barbed wire sprung loose from the stretching machine and slammed into his leg. The pain, God, the pain. It was like twenty knives stabbing him in the thigh. He saw himself stumbling toward the pickup, then driving into town, weaving along the road. Before the lights went out, a big fat tree loomed ahead.

Down below his waist, in a region meant for pleasure, something throbbed that shouldn't. "How bad?" he asked Claire and tried to move his leg.

"Bad. But you'll live, if you keep that leg still." She turned to Lila. "I'll finish the dressings."

"I'll be next door if you need me."

Dugan heard the door open and close again. No more of Lila's grating voice. Only the ticking of a clock. A gust of wind rattling tree branches against a window. And Claire standing at the side of the bed, lifting the sheet aside and staring down at . . . his private parts.

What had he done to himself anyway?

With the tips of her fingers, she poked and prodded the skin way up on his thigh dangerously close to his male appendage. Her poking hurt —

102

and it didn't. He could tell her hands were trembling. Why?

"Don't move a muscle unless I tell you," she said.

If she touched him again—there—he'd move a muscle all right, or it would move all by its lonely self. Thinking more clearly now, he decided he'd better talk to distract himself and his independently thinking appendage. "What's the damage, Doc?"

"You punctured your femoral artery." She pointed to the juncture of his right thigh and his groin. "And you've got a bunch of nasty scratches, which Lila just finished abrading."

"So that's what she was doing. I thought she was setting my leg on fire."

"This should make it feel better. Salve." With gloved hands she squeezed a blob of white onto her fingertips. Even through the thin rubber coating he could feel the heaven of her touch—and her trembling fingers.

Dugan gazed down his flattened torso and grinned. "Hey, Doc?"

She glanced up with a puzzled look. "Yes?"

"Got a question for you."

"What do you want to know?"

"Are you nervous working around down there?"

She lifted her chin a fraction and a wash of pink colored her cheeks. "Of course not. I'm a doctor. I do this all the time."

"All the time, huh?"

"Sure."

103

"When you do it all the time, do your hands shake?"

She wouldn't look at him, wouldn't meet his eyes for a second. She merely ducked her head and muttered, "No. It's . . . a little cool in here."

He wiggled his hand free from a terry cloth loop and ran an open palm across his bare chest. He shot a monkey grin at the doc. "Not cool to me." He snagged her free hand and flattened it over his chest. "See? No goose bumps."

She snatched her hand away, still refusing to meet his gaze. But he could tell she was fighting a grin.

Good. He was finally getting somewhere.

"You want to tell me how you did this?" she asked.

If Claire wished to pretend he was any old patient, he'd go along with the ruse. He'd seen what he needed to see. He could still get a reaction from her, which meant there was hope.

"I bought some more feeder cattle last week. The darned fools have been getting out and tramping Joseph Witcomb's sweet potatoes. So I decided I'd better string barbed wire around the pasture. You remember that gizmo I use that stretches the prickly stuff from one post to the other, don't you?"

She nodded. "They call it a comealong, don't they?"

"That's it."

Claire finished her doctoring in what became jerky, flustered movements. Dugan tried not to smile while he explained how the comealong had malfunctioned. How one minute he'd been working on the confounded apparatus with a screwdriver and the next disimpaling himself from the barbed wire that had snapped loose and whipped into his leg. He vaguely remembered stumbling to his pickup and driving into town.

"You're going to need a good week in bed—and a new pickup, I'm afraid."

He groaned against his pillow. "I just bought her a couple months ago."

"It's only money, Dugan." She peeled the gloves from her hands and dropped them into a waste basket by his bed. Then she drew his crisp white sheet over a tent device erected over his wounds.

Only money. Claire was right. A wrecked pickup was a small price to pay for a week of Claire tending to his ailing body. Smoothing salve over his wounds—there—with silky fingers. Hmm. He chuckled and was sorry. "Ouch!"

"I told you to lie still."

Sure, Doc. Tell that to my friend down there.

She sat in a rocking chair beside his bed and smoothed her hair behind her ear. She had masses of gorgeous, blond wavy hair, the kind a man liked to wad into his fists when he hovered over a woman's body.

The blond still looked natural and as silky as that Persian kitten's that had delivered a fresh litter in his barn. Maybe Claire would like to drop by and see the new kittens. Maybe they'd wind up rolling in the hay.

Uh-oh. You again. Lie down and rest. No? Damn! "Ouch!"

"Dugan, you're simply going to have to get a grip."

"Doc, if you only knew how funny that was from my perspective."

Pretending—he was sure she was pretending—she didn't have a clue what he was talking about, she folded her hands in her lap. Her long graceful fingers had once worked magic on his aching muscles. Maybe, if he was extra nice, he could talk her into a massage. Nurses gave massages. Did doctors?

"You shouldn't do such dangerous work alone. Dugan, do you realize you could have killed yourself?"

"But I didn't." He grinned. "You saved me."

"Dugan . . ."

"My men were either sick or knee deep in chores. If I didn't repair the fence, the cattle would have scattered by now to kingdom come. And Joseph would be madder than a wet hen. Thanks for pulling me through, Doc."

She smiled softly, the old Claire smile he'd conjured up in his dreams. "My pleasure."

"Huh-uh. Mine."

Then she did what in his estimation was something strange, even if his vision and thinking were beginning to play tricks on him.

She gripped the arms of her chair and rocked hard, her lips clamped shut. She rocked, and she rocked, and she rocked.

106

"Something on your mind, Doc?" he finally asked.

The rocking abruptly ceased. She licked her lips and regarded him with an open, questioning stare. "Why did you send me away?"

Her question nailed him as deeply as the barbed wire. What the hell had he said in his delirium to prompt her to ask that, and how could he answer? He decided to say as little as he could get away with. "You know why."

"You stopped loving me, right?"

"Something like that."

"I want to hear you say it. I want to hear you say, 'I packed your bags and loaded you on that bus because I didn't love you anymore.' Come on, Dugan. Say it."

He pretended to yawn and let his eyelids drift shut. "Later, Doc. I'm awful tired."

"Oh, no, you don't." She gripped his forearm with nails sharp enough to leave half moons in his flesh. "Open your eyes, Dugan Nichols. We're going to talk this out."

"I thought we agreed to forgive and forget all that," he said by way of diversion.

"That was before I heard you rambling in your sleep."

"I'm sure I didn't mean what I said, whatever it was."

"Dugan, you haven't answered my question. Why did you send me away?"

"The truth, I suppose."

"Unvarnished, please."

"You aren't going to like it."

"Try me."

"You won't hit me, will you?" he procrastinated.

One corner of her mouth lifted in a half grin. "Not in your present condition."

"Okay, here goes." He took a deep breath and searched for the words to explain what he'd done. He had never wanted her to find out what she was forcing him to say. Knowing Claire though, he realized that if he'd even hinted at the truth in his delirium, she wouldn't rest until she knew all of it. "You were sick."

"Yes."

"Horrible sick. You were nothing but skin and bones."

"Skin and bones," she repeated. "Yes, go on."

"After Angela died, it was like your spirit died, and your body was trying to join up with it. I saw you slipping away from me, day by day. Your eyes lost their sparkle. You hardly spoke. Claire, I was afraid I was going to lose you like we lost Angela."

"Lose me? That doesn't make sense. You lost me when you sent me away."

"In a way yes, in a way no."

"But why didn't you just—"

"I tried to get you to move into town with Lila so you could rest up. Put some weight back on."

"You needed me on the farm. My place was there with you."

"I needed you alive. I was going nuts trying to figure out what to do. Then one day I found you

108

behind the house, reading a letter. It was the letter that said you only had one more year to accept your scholarship, or that college in Pennsylvania would cancel the offer."

"How did you know about that letter?"

"I watched you cry. The tears streamed down your face. I'd always respected your privacy, but I had to know what was hurting you so. I waited until you fell asleep. Then I snuck out of bed and searched the house until I found the letter."

"Under the bread box."

"After I read it, I hated myself. If it hadn't been for me, you would have been studying at that college. You wouldn't have got pregnant. You wouldn't have almost died delivering Angela. You wouldn't have ruined your chances of having the babies you wanted. You wouldn't have almost wasted away pining for Angela."

Claire bit her lip. The tears crested her lids to streak over her cheeks. Dugan wanted to hold her in his arms and tell her he was sorry. But all he could do was say, "Claire, I did what I did because I loved you."

Her chin shot up. Fire leapt to the blue of her eyes. "What I want to know is, who appointed you God?" She stood and paced the length of the bed beside him in hard, angry strides. "Who gave you the right to decide what was best for me?"

"You weighed ninety pounds when you left, Claire — ninety pounds! Your clothes, no, your skin hung on you. Now look at you. You're a fine, healthy woman. You're a doctor. You save lives.

You saved mine. That was what you were supposed to do. You weren't meant to waste away on a grubby dirt farm with a husband who couldn't give you anything but grief."

She swiped at her tears with the back of her hand and shook her head. "If only Orville had given us that loan we begged him for."

"I guess only a fool would loan a man money who was up to his ears in debt."

"He lent you the money after I left. Why? Because he finally satisfied the grudge he'd been carrying against my father by getting rid of me?"

"I don't think so. Things just started to happen after you left. His son got into trouble. John needed help. I needed an extra hand. I finally hit a string of good luck."

"Why didn't you answer my letters?"

"Because," he said, meeting Claire's accusing gaze, "I knew if I did, you'd read the love between the lines."

"Oh, Dugan."

"You'd give up your dreams and come back, and I'd wind up hurting you all over again."

"I wanted you more than I wanted to become a doctor, but you didn't give me that choice."

"I'm not sorry for what I did. I did what was best for you. Now I hope you'll give us another chance. A chance to get to know the people we are now. We could start over, Claire. It isn't too late."

The old Claire would have grabbed the water from the nightstand and dumped it in his face. She would have stood at the foot of his bed and given him the verbal lashing of his life. She would have slammed out of the room and left him fuming.

But this Claire, the new Claire, stood there staring at him for so long his vision started to blur. Then she slid her hands into the pockets of her white coat and crossed to the window. She drew aside the curtain and stared out into the street, saying nothing. He thought he detected a hint of melancholy on her face, but he couldn't tell for sure.

Lord, what had he done by sending her away? Turned a sweet, loving thing into this iceberg of a woman?

"Well?" he finally prompted her.

She let the curtain fall from her fingertips, then leaned back against the wall, her arms crossed beneath her breasts. "I don't know what to say."

"You don't? Maybe you didn't hear me. I just proposed, Claire. I just asked you, in my own way, if we could pick up where we left off, and that's your response? 'I don't know what to say?' What about, 'Go to hell?' What about, 'Give me time to think about it?' What about—" he paused, the room's dimensions warped in his vision "—what about, 'Yes, Dugan, I want to be your wife?'"

She glanced at him briefly, as if he were a fly on the wall or a patient who didn't need her attention. A huge, burning knot swelled in Dugan's throat. His heart thumped so loud he was sure she could hear it galloping in his chest like a frisky colt's.

Say the words, Claire. Say the words I long to hear. It's not too late. We can start over.

"I don't know, Dugan," she answered on a plaintive sigh. "So much has happened. There's been so much hurt, so many lies. We're older. We've changed. It just may be too late for us."

Lord in heaven, what had he done to the woman he loved?

Chapter Six

While her insides tumbled out of control, Claire somehow maintained a cool facade so she wouldn't upset Dugan any more than necessary. Fortunately, the pain medication kicked in, and he sank into a deep and troubled sleep.

If she hadn't been a doctor, she would have flung his half-baked marriage proposal in his face and told him he was twelve years too late. However, she knew that such a retort would have endangered his condition.

She summoned Lila to the room and escaped to the privacy of the hallway. The world was spinning without her, somewhere off in space. She was caught up between the present and the past, events and words colliding in her mind like frantic, caged birds.

The string of acceptance she'd wound around her heart to cope with Dugan's rejection unraveled at a dizzying rate. His confession had propelled her back to those weeks before he'd put her on the bus to Philadelphia. All the pain and confusion . . . the rejection . . . she'd endured hit her full force, as if she were living it all over again.

Her logical physician's mind prescribed time alone to sort truth from fabrication. Still in a daze, she wandered downstairs to the registration desk. She rented another room. Dugan could have her suite. She wanted to be as far away from him as possible.

Her new room, on the hotel's back side, was a cramped single that hadn't been rented in months. It was scheduled for renovation. Claire didn't care if the furniture hadn't been dusted, if the air conditioner, idle for weeks, hadn't filtered the dust and humidity from the air.

As she closed the door, her pretense of composure shattered. Leaning back against the seasoned wood, she crossed her arms over her chest and gave in to the trembling grief that seized her.

Even in the stagnant heat of mid-August, she shivered from the cold—the cold, awful truth Dugan had just dumped on her like a load of manure from his pasture.

Don't let him do this to you again. He can't hurt you if you don't let him.

Attempting to regain control, she took deep gulps of the dusty air and flung herself across the bed. But the moment her head hit the pillow, the sobbing began. She thought of all the years she and Dugan could have shared, if only he'd told her the truth then, instead of now.

He'd been so good at pretending he didn't love her that she'd believed every word he'd said. Believed him when he told her, with a stony look of indifference, that his love had died after they'd lost Angela.

How could any man do that to the woman he loved?

A gentle rapping sounded at the door. "Claire? Claire? Are you in there? It's only me, Lila."

"Please, leave me alone. I'm . . . tired. So tired," she ended on a whisper. She blew her reddened nose into a tissue. Maybe Lila would get the hint and go away.

Not Lila. She bustled in, two aspirins in one hand and a glass of water in the other. She plunked all three onto the nightstand. "Here, take these."

"But I—"

"Doctor's orders."

"But I'm the doctor."

"And one very disillusioned young lady, I imagine."

Suddenly bitterness was the only emotion left for Claire to deal with. Her voice sounded cold and brittle as she spoke. "Dugan told you."

"After you left." Lila hitched a hip across Claire's bed and smoothed damp wisps of hair off her cheeks. For a moment Claire was a young girl, and Lila was her mother, doling out her precious combination of good sense and affection.

"He's up there wallowing in his guilt about now," Lila said.

"Good. I hope he suffers."

"Like you suffered?"

"Nobody deserves this kind of pain. Aunt Lila, he broke my heart. He says he did it because he loved me. That doesn't make sense."

"Oh, I don't know, child. Maybe if you'd been hunkerin' on the other side of the fence like he was, you might've done likewise."

"Never. Not in a million years."

Lila smiled softly and handed her a fresh tissue. "Never's a pretty rigid word."

"I'd never send the man I love away."

"Do you love him still, Claire? Do you wake up thinkin' about him? Do you remember times—good times? Do you remember when you made love?"

Claire heaved a shuddering sigh. "Yes. Yes. How can I forget—if only I could!"

"But you're sendin' the man away, so to speak."

"What do you expect me to do?"

"That's not for me to say. I'm just pointin' out a discrepancy in your thinkin'."

"How do I know he isn't lying? He lied to me once. Maybe he's doing it again. Maybe, because I'm back in town, healthy and earning a good

116

living, he's decided I wouldn't be a liability anymore."

Lila glanced away for a moment, then back again. "I wasn't supposed to tell anybody this, but there's something you ought to know about your bein' here and all."

"If it's all the same to you, I've had all the revelations I can take for one day."

"Well, you're going to hear one more. You see, if it weren't for Dugan, you wouldn't have got the job here."

"What do you mean?"

"I mean—and if you ever tell anyone I told you this, I'll tell 'em you dreamed it up—I mean, when we voted, the board deadlocked. Twice. Dugan, bein' chairman and all, had to break the tie. He picked you, Claire, and endured some pretty tough criticism, I might add. So, in a way, you could say you owe your windfall to the man you're shootin' poison darts at."

"And I'm supposed to feel grateful. Well, pardon me, I don't. Surprised, yes. Grateful, no."

Claire shook her head. "Now, on top of everything else, I find out I didn't exactly have a mandate for the job. Aunt Lila, I love you like a mother, but I didn't need that from you today."

"The truth hurts sometimes, but it helps clear up fuzzy thinkin'. You needed to know Dugan was sincere when he sent you away. He wanted to give you a chance to grab your golden ring. By votin' you director, he finished what he started twelve years ago. Stupid as his decision was to put you on that bus without your say-so, he did in his heart what he thought was good for you. There wasn't a selfish bone in that man's body.

"I know you hurt, but think about him. What he went through. The sacrifice. Give the man credit for givin' up the thing he loved the most."

"The golden ring," Claire repeated, rubbing the bare skin on her wedding finger. "He gave me the chance for one, but he took the other off my finger. He had no right."

Lila bent over and kissed her cheek. "I can see you need some time for thinkin'."

Her chin quivering, Claire could only nod. She wondered how many years of thinking it would take before she accepted what had happened to her, to her marriage . . . and yes, to Dugan.

"Don't worry about Dugan," Lila said as she stood. "Your days of nursin' him are over—if that's how you want it to be."

That's how Claire wanted it, all right.

She delegated the hour-to-hour care-giving to Lila and the two clinic nurses. In their capable hands, Dugan miraculously survived the third critical day in healing without any complications.

He moved home at the end of the week, with strict instructions from Claire. He wasn't to lift

118

anything heavier than five pounds for four more weeks to keep the artery from rupturing.

Every Monday Claire drove out to the ranch to check his wounds, each time making sure the matronly housekeeper he'd hired was by her side. If Claire was alone with Dugan, and he so much as kissed her on the cheek, she was afraid all the need would bubble up, and she'd leap straight into his arms.

Or, she thought, as she gazed across the cluttered construction site behind the clinic, she'd smack him in the mouth with a closed fist.

"That's going to be some house, Dr. Linwood."

Claire snapped out of her reverie and smiled at Pamela Sue. All about them carpenters and brick masons and electricians were working overtime to build Claire's very own house. A two-story Queen Anne Victorian with balconies and turrets and a front porch where someday she could rock away her retirement years.

Alone.

She sighed into the September wind. If only Pamela Sue knew her ambivalent feelings about moving into that house. Sure, she couldn't wait to own her home. But she and Dugan used to sit on the porch in the evenings and talk about their dream house that never came to be. Claire hadn't counted on those conversations echoing in the empty rooms as this house was built. She wished she could rid her thoughts of Dugan and be done with him.

"After the baby comes, you'll have to stop by," she told the teenager. "Stay over, if you like."

She shrugged to think the lovely house would always be only a house and not a home. The laughter of her own children would never echo off walls and down the stairway as she'd always dreamed.

Pamela Sue smoothed her hands over her swollen belly and gave a wan smile. "Sometimes I think this baby'll never get here."

"Let's see. Only six more weeks to go—right?"

The crunch of feet on gravel sounded behind them. Claire glanced over her shoulder and saw Dugan ambling over, his thumbs hooked in the front pockets of his jeans. She squeezed her car keys until the metal dug into her palm. What was he doing there?

"Well, hi, Dugan," Pamela Sue said, waddling over to greet him. "You're looking fit."

Dugan spoke to her, but his gaze was fixed on Claire. "As Fred says, I feel fine as frog hairs—thanks to the doc there."

Pamela Sue glanced from Dugan to Claire and back again and grinned knowingly. "Um, well, I—I'd best be getting back to the clinic."

"Don't forget to lie down and rest your back," Claire told her.

"I will," the girl said, backing across the lot as if she suspected something romantic was about to happen which she didn't want to miss. "Have fun!"

"Dear Lord, to think that child's going to be a mother herself," Claire said, self-consciously fluttering her hand at the departing teenager.

"She'll do fine, because she has you. You'll see."

"So, what brings you to town?" Claire asked and heard the brittle quality in her own voice.

"Moses finished getting the kinks out of my pickup."

"You didn't have to buy a new one after all?"

"Huh-uh. She's ready to roll."

"And your leg's healed well enough to drive it."

"You bet it has." He spread his arms wide. "I wouldn't object if you wanted to check me over one more time."

"In your dreams," she mumbled under her breath. She glanced away lest he detect the longing that sprang to her abdomen the moment she saw him sauntering across the lot.

"In my dreams is right," he said pointedly. "But, Doc?"

"Yes?"

"At least I got you to smile."

"I smile all the time."

"Funny. That's not what I hear."

"Oh, what do you hear?"

"That you've been a bit down in the mouth lately." He meandered closer, so close she could

121

smell the splash of lemony cologne emanating from his neck. "And you sure don't smile when you see me."

Why did he have to be so damned perceptive? Claire asked herself. And so disquietingly attractive?

She let her gaze linger on his strong, square jaw, a legacy from his grandfather, who'd raised him after his parents had abandoned him; on the dark, well-sculpted brows that shaded brown eyes studying her with unveiled interest. She hoped like heck he couldn't detect the telltale thump-thumping beneath her lab coat.

She didn't want to react this way when she was with Dugan. She wanted to put her feelings and memories of him to rest finally and unequivocally. As Lila said, though, she supposed that would take time.

Dugan glanced over her shoulder. "Heard about your house from Orville."

She whirled around, relieved at the new turn in the conversation. "What do you think?"

"Truth?"

"Of course."

"It's an awful lot of house for one woman. Course you must be sick of living in that hotel."

"You can say that again."

"You know, you didn't have to go build a house."

Claire frowned at him. "There wasn't anything available. I had to."

122

"You could come live with me anytime you want."

And send her away again if he decided she'd be better off. No way. Not again. "Dugan . . ."

"All right." His Adam's apple bobbed up and down over a smoothly shaved neck. He glanced at the toe of his boots before regarding her with a determined look. "I'll leave it alone . . . for now. But I'm serving you notice. I'm not giving up on you, Doc. And I'm sure as hell not giving up on us."

"Suit yourself."

"I usually do."

"Indeed," she murmured.

Feeling the need to put some breathing room between them, Claire forced a smile and turned to lead him on a tour of her house.

The tour was a mistake. Dugan followed her through the front door and made a great pretense of examining a seam in the wallboard before he hit her with another well-aimed missile.

"This house must be setting you back a good piece. Payments. Insurance. Furniture."

"I can afford it," she maintained, bristling.

"And the car, too?"

She held her breath a long time to avoid telling him he could go take a flying leap. "Dugan," she said, sugar sweetly, "my personal finances are none of your business. You gave up that right —"

"Twelve years ago. I probably should have kept

my mouth shut. But, well—as a friend now, just as a friend, nothing more—it seems to me you're digging yourself into a mighty big hole of debt."

"You write my checks. You should know I can afford all this and more."

"My grandfather thought he could afford to pay off his debts, too."

"He got carried away with borrowing. I won't make that mistake."

He flashed that dimpled grin, darn him. Whether or not she wanted her resentment to fade away, his teasing nature banished her antagonism. They stood there in what would one day be her kitchen, their faces bathed in the sunset slanting through the window.

Sunset—Claire's favorite time of day.

Unbidden, memories of their playful teasing in the kitchen on the farm surfaced.

"I always did like the way you looked with the sun in your hair . . . on your cheeks. Hmm." Dugan reached up and touched her cheek softly, tentatively.

Claire froze in place, afraid to move for fear she'd glide right into his arms.

"Pretty. Pretty, pretty woman."

The pager on Claire's belt beeped annoyingly.

"Duty calls," she whispered, yet she didn't move away from Dugan—not one inch.

"Yeah," he said, slinging a bold arm around her shoulder and heading toward the door in that slow, sexy saunter of his. "Duty has a way of doing that, doesn't it?"

Claire lay awake in bed that night, trying to ignore the knot of need in her stomach. One minute she pictured herself railing at Dugan for criticizing her spending habits. The next she was standing next to him in her kitchen, feeling the moistness of his minty breath on her uplifted face.

Why couldn't he leave her alone?

The phone on her nightstand jangled. Welcoming the intrusion, she lifted the receiver on the second ring. "Dr. Linwood."

"Doc," Fred mumbled into the phone in a sleepy voice, "you've got a long distance call, collect."

"Where from?"

"Mexico."

"Mexico? I don't know anyone in Mexico."

"Orville and Ruthie's down there. S'pose it could be them?"

"I guess," she agreed. "Put the call through."

After what seemed like an interminable series of clicks and transfers, the refined voice of the bank president's wife trembled over the line. "D-Dr. L-Linwood—Claire, th-this is R-Ruthie."

"Yes, Ruthie. What's wrong?"

"It's Orville." Her word caught on a poorly stifled sob. "I think he's had a h-heart attack."

Claire had recently given Orville a complete

physical. His complications were numerous: a hiatal hernia, high blood pressure, and gout. The prescribed treatment involved a special diet and regimen of medication difficult to manage. Still, his EKG had been normal. She grabbed a pad and pen to make notes.

"Calm down, Ruthie. Tell me everything you know. First, where are you?"

"The Palacio Hotel."

"Have you contacted the hotel doctor?"

"He isn't here. No one seems to know how to find him. No one's in a hurry to do anything around this place," she wailed.

"What are Orville's symptoms?"

"This afternoon he didn't feel well. I thought he was getting, you know, the *turistas,* so I gave him an antacid tablet and made him lie down. He said he was sure it wasn't anything serious, probably the papaya juice he drank at lunch causing his hiatal hernia to act up."

"Is he experiencing any chest pain?"

"Some."

"Pain in his arm?"

"He hasn't complained of that."

"Has he vomited, Ruthie?"

"Yes."

"How many times?"

"Once. And, Claire, his face is gray and clammy. What are we going to do?"

"I'll see if I can locate someone competent to check on him," Claire said, but even as she spoke she knew the task wouldn't be easy. "Keep Orville calm and don't feed him anything until you hear from me. And, Ruthie?"

"Yes?"

"Try to remain calm for Orville's sake, and stay by the phone. I'll call you back within the hour."

An hour. An hour was an eternity for anyone who'd suffered a heart attack. Orville should have been transported to a hospital within thirty minutes of the first symptoms. With his health complications, why had he flown to Cancún without checking out the medical community there in advance?

Claire gave up trying to reach a doctor through the operator at the hotel. At night apparently only a skeleton staff was on duty, and that didn't include an English-speaking concierge.

Her calls to the local hospital were equally frustrating. No one seemed to understand Orville needed emergency treatment, and fast.

She dialed every physician she knew in Texas border towns, but no one could recommend a doctor within thirty miles of Cancún. She tried several Lubbock travel agencies, hoping they could refer her to a competent physician, but no one answered.

The next best thing she knew was to fly down

herself. She threw a few clothes into a suitcase and grabbed her medical bag. She cringed at the thought of the hour-and-a-half's drive into Lubbock, then God only knows how long she'd have to wait to make connections into Cancún.

If Orville didn't get oxygen and something for the chest pain, he could suffer further damage to his heart. In the worst scenario, he might even die. No matter how much she disliked the man, she didn't wish him an early death, or Ruthie the anguish.

She phoned the Palacio Cancún and told Ruthie she was on her way. She would call from the airport when she knew her arrival time.

Next she awoke the kindly pediatrician in Amarillo who'd applied for her job. He actually sounded excited about covering for her while she was away.

She'd just opened her door to leave when the phone rang again. After a moment's hesitation, she grabbed the receiver and said, "Dr. Linwood. Please, make this quick. I have a medical emergency."

"Doc? This is Dugan. What's up?"

"It's Orville. Ruthie called from their hotel in Cancún. I'm afraid Orville's had a heart attack."

"Jesus, what are you going to do?"

"They can't find a doctor. I tried to locate one myself, but I've come up empty-handed. I was on my way out the door. I'm going to drive to Lubbock and catch the next flight down."

"You'd do that for Orville, with the bad blood between you?"

"I'm a doctor. Bad blood or not, he's my patient, and he needs me."

"Looks like we hired the right doctor," Dugan told her, the admiration evident in his voice. "Don't go driving into Lubbock. I can fly you to Cancún ten times quicker'n you can get there on the commercial birds."

"Dugan, it's a long flight."

"I've flown longer. I've got tip tanks on the wings. Besides, we'll refuel in Brownsville when I file my international flight plan. I'll be fueled up and ready to go by the time you get here."

"I can't tell you how much I appreciate this."

"I'll call your aunt. If we fly Orville back, she could come in handy, and she's always on alert."

"Honestly," Claire said, grabbing her purse and suitcase, "if you were here right now, I'd kiss you so hard, your teeth would fall out!"

Dugan was an exceptional pilot. In the black of night he lifted the King Air turbo prop off his blacktop runway and streaked south to Brownsville for a brief stop.

After the group of three took off from Brownsville, Claire sat in the copilot's seat and listened to him squawk a code into the transponder so they could penetrate the U.S. Air Defense System.

Flying at 22,000 feet, they covered the distance to Cancún in just under two-and-a-half hours. Lila was reading, and Claire was nodding to the high-pitched whine of the engines when Dugan radioed his approach and eased his plane onto the runway as if he flew every day of his life.

Just before the sun transformed the dark Caribbean waters into glittering turquoise seas, Dugan taxied onto a ramp to park at what he called a fixed base operator. As far as Claire could tell, it looked like a glorified gas station for planes.

She paced like a nervous cat while they endured the slow pace of the customs officials. Because the group hadn't flown under the discerning eye of a commercial airline, the inspectors poked and prodded every bag. They were especially interested in the valise containing Claire's medications and the trunk packed with the portable EKG.

Claire, Dugan, and Lila found a cabby asleep in his Volkswagen. Twenty thousand pesos and twenty minutes later, they swerved up the circle driveway fronting the luxurious hotel near the far end of the ocean-view strip.

The Palacio Cancún gazed east over the Caribbean like a regal Mayan princess. Even as the sun peeked over the ocean's horizon, the wait staff strolled though the open-air restaurant off the main lobby. They were readying buffet tables laden with native fruits and freshly baked breads. The aromas made even Claire think of breakfast for a fleeting moment.

Finally, on the fifteenth floor, they followed a frigidly air-conditioned corridor outside to a connecting wing of suites.

Claire glanced at her watch. Four hours had passed since Dugan had pulled back the rudder and glided his plane into the West Texas sky. She prayed she wasn't too late.

Ruthie answered the door wearing a red and yellow floral duster and a worried frown. "Thank God you're here," she told Claire, grabbing her hand and pulling her inside.

Claire followed Orville's wife over a pink marble entry, up a steeply winding staircase to the second floor of the suite. To the right was a pink marble hot tub, powder room, and bathroom. To the left, a master bedroom bigger than Claire's efficiency back in Philadelphia. Across the entire back wall of the second floor was a wall of curtained windows that opened onto a broad patio.

Orville lay in the center of a king-sized bed, looking small and insignificant, as he stared at the ceiling. He greeted Claire with a weak wave and a wan smile.

While Lila fussed with his pillow, Claire stepped into the bathroom to scrub away the trip's dirt and a fine layer of powdery sand. Dugan stood in the open doorway, giving Ruthie a sorely needed propping up.

"Any change since we spoke?" Claire asked her.

"He's still the same."

"Has he slept?"

"About an hour."

"Dugan," she said over Ruthie's shoulder, "would you take Ruthie down for a bite to eat while I examine Orville? Aunt Lila's going to stay here with me."

"Sure thing, Doc." He winked at Claire and offered Ruthie his arm. "And if you're lucky, we'll bring you back some of those mouth-watering pastries."

Ruthie paused to say good-bye to her husband, moving to his side and wringing his hand. "I won't be gone more'n twenty minutes, dear."

"Take your time, honey," Orville said, but Claire didn't think he meant it by the reluctant way in which he let go of his wife's hand.

"Don't worry about Ruthie," Dugan assured Orville. "I'll take good care of her until the doc here's done her thing."

As soon as the door clicked shut behind Dugan and Ruthie, Orville's hoarse voice echoed across the room. "I told Ruthie I didn't think you'd come."

"Why wouldn't I?" Claire asked perfunctorily, while she moved her stethoscope over his chest.

"One hell of a house call, for one thing."

"If I had to make a house call, I couldn't

132

think of a lovelier place. Now, shh. I want to listen to you breathe, Orville."

"I suppose you know I voted against hiring you."

"No, I didn't," she replied, thinking the bigger surprise would have been if he had voted in her favor. "But whether you did or didn't is beside the point. I'm your doctor, and I'm here. I'll give you something for the pain. Then we're going to hook you up to the oxygen."

"Plus there's that business about your daddy," Orville persisted.

Claire's hands stilled for only the slightest moment as she continued her examination. She looked up at Lila, who shot her a knowing glance. Claire was determined not to let bad blood between her family and Orville's affect her attitude toward her needy patient. "I don't know what you mean."

"Don't be coy with me, Doc. There hasn't been any love lost between us since your daddy flunked . . . that is, since John flunked high school physics."

Claire would have been a fool to miss his change in emphasis—in blame, to be more precise. "Orville, what's in the past is in the past." She smiled reassuringly and meant it. "Right now, I'm only concerned with your health. Is this the first time you've suspected you were having trouble with your heart?"

"I've been having a speck of indigestion after

133

eating lunch every day. I just thought it was Imogene's meat loaf." He pressed a fist to his ample girth. "Green peppers do it every time."

"I'm afraid we're dealing with more than green peppers and meat loaf. But speaking of eating, once we patch you up, I want you to drop a few pounds."

"Wait'll Ruthie hears. She's been badgering me to lose weight for years. Guess now I'll have to listen."

"I brought along a portable EKG. I'm going to hook you up so I can see what we're dealing with here. Afterward, we'll talk. Aunt Lila, you want to give me a hand?"

"Doc?" Orville said.

"Yes?"

"I got to get something off my chest first."

"This isn't a confessional, Orville. I'm going to check your heart, not your conscience."

"Maybe one has something to do with the other."

"Oh, how is that?"

"Maybe I'm paying for the error of my ways."

Claire sat on the edge of the bed and waited. This wasn't the first time a patient had feared meeting his Maker and wanted to clear his conscience. Precious minutes were ticking away. But if she rushed Orville, she might trigger his anxiety. She waited for what she expected would be a King Midas confession about a lifetime of worshipping money.

"I wish your daddy was still alive."

"What would you do if he were?"

"Make apologies to both of you."

"What apologies, Orville?"

"For blaming him—and you, after he died, bless his departed soul—for the problems my son, John, got himself into."

"Oh, that," she said flatly. "That was a long time ago."

"It was so easy to blame somebody else. Anger burned in my gut when John lost his college scholarship. I blamed your daddy because John flunked physics."

"Daddy only gave him the grade he deserved," Claire said in defense of her father.

"I wish I could have seen that back then. Instead I let my rage eat me up like an ulcer. After your daddy died, I couldn't hurt him, so I did the next best thing. I hurt you." He clutched the sheet's crisp hem tightly in his hands. "If I'd loaned you and Dugan the money you asked for—"

"We might have defaulted on the loan," she said, taking pity on the repentant man. She worried about the effect of his rambling confession on his physical condition.

"No, let me finish. This is something I got to do."

"If it will make you feel better," she said, but in truth she didn't want to hear any more. She didn't want anyone else churning up the emotions she was having a difficult time putting to rest.

"If I'd given you young folks the loan—" Orville's voice cracked "—maybe that sweet baby wouldn't have died. Maybe you wouldn't have up and left Dugan. Maybe he wouldn't have turned into a grouchy old hermit and made himself miserable."

It wasn't that Claire didn't appreciate Orville's apology after all these years, especially for her father's sake, but she did not want to discuss losing Angela. Every time someone said her baby's name, a raw sore opened up inside Claire.

She also did not want to talk about poor Dugan's misery after she left. She was sick and tired of hearing how he'd suffered. If only the folks of Sierra knew what poor Dugan had done to bring the misery on himself!

As luck would have it, she could do nothing but assure Orville he'd acted like a protective father. She turned away, pretending to look for something in her medical kit so Orville couldn't see the resentment burning in her eyes.

"I'm not so old I can't see," Orville continued, and Lila rolled her eyes, "that you still care for your hus—excuse me—for the man who used to be your husband. If you'll leave us alone when he gets back with Ruthie, I'll put in a good word for you."

"That won't be necessary, Orville," she replied and patted his shoulder reassuringly. "What happened between me and Dugan was a long time ago. We're different people now. He's got his life. I've got mine. I don't want you to think I don't appreciate what you're offering to do. But, please, just relax and let Lila and me take care of you."

Dugan sat on the sitting room couch, squeezing Ruthie's clammy hand in a comforting gesture.

Poor Ruthie hadn't been able to eat a bite. Now that Claire had finished examining Orville, she was ready to explain her findings to Ruthie.

Dugan only hoped the news wasn't as bad as Ruthie feared.

"Orville's had a heart attack, Ruthie, but a mild one."

"I guess I should be thankful for that."

"I was wondering," Claire continued. "Has Orville used that hot tub upstairs this week?"

"Why we both have," Ruthie said with a downward flutter of her lashes.

Dugan sensed the embarrassment in the flush of pink on the woman's face. He wondered if Claire knew how hard Ruthie had worked on Orville to leave the bank and go on this vacation. It was their first trip out of the country.

"How long did you stay in the tub, with the jets on?" Claire asked.

"Forty-five minutes. Maybe an hour." Ruthie

rolled the hem of her dress in her lap. "I've never been in a hot tub before."

"Forty-five minutes? Hmm. That may have been Orville's problem."

"You mean a hot tub can cause a heart attack?"

"Sometimes, especially if you stay in too long in water too deep."

"A heart attack," Ruthie whimpered. "What are we going to do?"

She looked first to Dugan, then back to the doc. Dugan gave Ruthie's drooping shoulders a reassuring squeeze and mouthed, "Are you all right?" to Claire. Her face was drawn, and she'd been acting strange since he brought back orange juice and chocolate croissants, along with Ruthie.

Claire's barely perceptible nod didn't fool Dugan. She was tired; she was hungry, and she was upset about something he was determined to find out about later.

"What I'd like to do is stabilize Orville first. I gave him something for the pain. Don't be upset when you see all the tubes. I've put him on oxygen and an IV to regulate his medication."

"Can he get out of bed?"

"Maybe this evening. After that, I'll want him to exercise. Walk mainly. Lila brought a suitcase full of food that'll be easier on his stomach than what he can find here. She also filled several gallon jugs with Sierra water. I don't want Orville drinking anything else. In four days we should be able to fly him to Lubbock, where he can see a heart specialist."

Ruthie's eyes grew as round as saucers. "Fly him? But wouldn't that be hard on his heart?"

"The plane's pressurized. I've flown heart patients before," Dugan assured her.

"Lila and I will take turns monitoring your husband. He's wearing a device that looks like a small transistor radio around his neck. That's a transmitter that will tell us if his heartbeat's irregular, something he may not realize himself."

"Can I see him now?"

"I think he'd like that, but he's a bit drowsy. When he gets home, he's going to have to learn to take things a whole lot easier."

"Just what I've been telling him," Ruthie maintained as she straightened her flowered dress. "Fool man spends his life at that bank."

Ruthie excused herself, leaving Claire alone with Dugan, a situation she had hoped to avoid.

"Nice job," Dugan told her and reached for her hand, but she jumped up from the couch and moved to the sliding glass door.

By now sun worshippers were stretching out on the lounges at the L-shaped pool behind the hotel. Even at this early hour, a white-coated bartender polished glasses behind the swim-up bar. A young Mexican boy with a round, happy face was doing a brisk business at the towel concession. Beyond, vacationers drifted down steps to a narrow strip of powdery white beach that fronted the ocean.

Claire opened the door and stepped out onto the balcony, drawing a deep breath of the humid, salty air. The turquoise surf rolled over the beach, delivering a frothy foam to the toes of children building sand castles.

"We've got a problem," Dugan said behind her.

Holding her breath, Claire turned to find him lounging against the balcony wall. He looked strangely out of place with his scuffed cowboy boots and well-worn jeans. She wondered if he'd still look as good in a swimsuit.

Right now a light sheen of perspiration shone on his tanned forehead and in the open neck of the yellow Western shirt he wore. He'd rolled up his sleeves to reveal the well-muscled arms of a farmer-rancher.

"What's the problem?"

"The hotel has one suite available, with two bedrooms, just down the hall."

"So, what's the problem?"

"I can't afford it."

Claire chuckled. "Yeah, right."

"No, I mean it. We left in such an all-fired hurry I didn't bring much money. And most of that I tipped to those boys in customs to hurry us through. I'll have to wire home before we can check in."

"No need." Claire moved into the sitting room and pulled a red leather billfold from her purse.

She took out a credit card and handed it to Dugan. "Put it on my card."

"I won't do that," he said, stubbornly lifting his chin.

"Don't be chauvinistic."

"I'm not being chauvinistic. I just don't want to charge the room. It's three hundred and fifty dollars a night. We could be here several days."

"If we're lucky," Claire said glancing backward at the beach, "I'm sure Orville'll reimburse us when we get back."

"I'll wire the bank for money."

"Here, give me that thing," she said, snatching the credit card from his fingers. "I'm going downstairs to check in before they give the room to someone else. Will you do me a favor and see what you can do about helping Lila?"

She crossed to the front door and turned to find him scowling back at her.

"I *will* wire for the money, Doc. And when we leave, there'll be cash on the counter — my cash. Not your credit card."

Chapter Seven

Claire got perverse pleasure charging the suite to her name, even if Dugan did intend to pay when they checked out.

He sulked while she moved about the upstairs bedroom of the suite, unpacking her clothes and toiletries. She did this in a precise and logical manner so she could dress quickly if called to Orville's side at a moment's notice.

She didn't own a decent swimsuit, and, knowing Dugan, she rather imagined he'd packed only the barest of necessities. "Come on," she said. "Lila insisted on taking the first shift. Let's go downstairs and buy some clothes."

"I don't need any clothes."

"Did you bring a swimsuit?"

"No. I don't have much call for one. When I swim in the pond, I just skinny-dip." He shot her a heavy-lidded glance. "Of course, you probably don't remember that, do you?"

Did she! She could still see his broad, even strokes, the sun reflecting off the corded muscles on his back as he cut the water with his arms. The first time he'd rolled onto his back, she'd blushed all the way to her toes. "You'll need a suit," she told him.

"And?"

"Something nice to wear when we go out to eat." She pulled a short black crepe cocktail dress from a straw shopping bag and reached for a hanger. "I spotted this in a boutique downstairs when I registered. You like it?"

He shot it a cursory look. "Nice, but I doubt you'll have a chance to wear it. We aren't on a vacation, Claire. We're here to take care of Orville."

"And we will. Lila and I have already talked it over. Orville's health comes first. But there's no reason we can't enjoy the surroundings while we're here. We're going to alternate shifts so we can all take in the sights. I brought my beeper and the base unit, so Lila can reach me at a moment's notice."

Claire angled the hanger containing the wisp of a dress before her and smiled. "Of course, if you don't want to join me, I'm sure I can find someone else who would be happy to take me—"

"The hell you say!"

Dugan strode across the room and snatched the dress from Claire's hands. He glared first at her, then at the garment. The skirt was short;

the neckline, plunging and what Claire called in-spiring.

"You really intend to wear this thing while you're here?" he demanded, his eyes glinting angrily.

"If I didn't, I wouldn't have bought it, now would I?"

"If you put that dress on, I'm going with you."

"Well, then," she countered coyly, "I guess we'd better hit the shops. A lady in the airport told me a man can't go into a decent restaurant at night in shorts or jeans."

"Then maybe we'll just have to eat in the inde-cent ones," Dugan groused.

"Suit yourself," she said, pivoting on her heel. She snapped up her purse from the chair and paused in the doorway leading to the circular stairs that descended to the suite's first floor.

"I suppose you're going to charge everything."

"But of course. Chill out, Dugan. We're in Cancún, Mexico. I, for one, do not intend to let a little thing like lack of cash ruin the trip. We may never get back here again. What do you say? Are you coming with me, or are you going to lie around this room all day and sulk?"

During their shopping expedition, Dugan felt like a calf trapped in a branding chute. Two young women with round, Mayan faces and

144

amused eyes helped Claire as she draped an end-
less array of shirts across his chest. Most of
them looked ugly enough to use for oil rags.

He refused to wear the Hawaiian print with
gaudy parrots squawking in palm trees. He did
agree on white cotton dress slacks like the ones
the locals were wearing around the hotel. Claire
also talked him into a white short-sleeved shirt.
When he got back to Sierra he'd rip out the stupid curly-cued embroidery that bordered its hem.

That, an okay pair of shorts, two T-shirts, and
a plain black swimsuit totaled two hundred dollars—two hundred! He hadn't paid that much
for clothes in three years. He ordered what he
needed from the Sears catalog. He bought
mostly jeans and a few work shirts, which he
paid for in cash, up front.

Claire's purchases were double his in dollars
but way prettier. She lingered over two turquoise
and silver bracelets, then said what the hell and
bought two—one for her and one for Lila.

She charged everything.

To his way of thinking, credit should be reserved for absolute emergencies, when a man
couldn't get his hand on cash. It shouldn't be
used for trinkets and clothes that brought a person nothing but pleasure and a hefty bill.

And, if he was any judge, that sweet, frugal
girl he'd married had pleasure on the mind—the
kind that cost a heap of money.

Dugan couldn't eat his lunch.

* * *

Claire's free time ran out before her credit card limit. She phoned Orville's room every hour to make sure he was resting well.

At 4:00 p.m. Dugan walked her to the Garrisons' suite for her eight-hour shift.

He'd planned on asking Lila if she wanted to go for a swim in the pool. But Lila had already persuaded Ruthie to join her for girl talk and a drink at the bar fronting the beach. That left Dugan free.

Free. Hell, he'd been free twelve years. Where he wanted to be was with Claire, especially at a time when that red flag of a credit card was nowhere in sight.

For lack of anything better to do, he rode the bus into town for a bargain fifty cents. Ten minutes from the hotel he spotted a sign for good-old American pizza and bounded off the bus. He brought back two large pepperonis with double cheese for dinner, which set him back less than twenty bucks. The spicy aroma filled the bus as he rode back with a proud, hungry grin.

He found a bottle of red wine, two stemmed glasses, and hors d'oeuvres on the bar in Orville and Ruthie's room.

"Did you order these?" he asked Claire.

"No, they come with the room every night."

"Want a glass?" he asked, gesturing to the wine.

"It's Ruthie's."

"We probably have the same tray in our room."

"Well, I guess we could replace it then. Sure, pour me a glass, but just one. I don't want to get sleepy while I'm watching over Orville."

Dugan poured the wine, handed a glass to Claire, and noticed she'd changed into a pink gauzy dress that bared her shoulders. When he'd left, she'd worn her hair tied back at her neck with a metal clip. Now it billowed about her head in a blond cloud.

She was a beautiful woman, and God knows she deserved the very best. All his life he'd promised himself if he ever had the chance with her again, he'd take her someplace nice, some-place exotic . . . someplace like Cancún.

Here they were, in just such a place, albeit under less-than-perfect conditions, and he was acting like a tightwad. He wouldn't complain anymore about her charging habits. At least he'd try not to until the money he'd wired home for arrived.

The money had better come, he thought, frowning. He'd planned a special night for them to share before they returned to Sierra. Before they returned to the memories that kept interfering with his efforts to get Claire back. The night he'd planned would cost a bundle of pesos. He'd be damned if he'd let Claire whip out her plastic card everywhere they went.

"Dugan?" she said in that lilting voice of hers.

"Yeah."

"A toast?"

"Um. Okay. Let's see." He clinked his glass to hers and thought for a moment. What could he say without making her dart away from him like a scared rabbit? "To . . . you."

He lifted his glass and gazed down into blue eyes whose beauty rivaled the ocean. A heady perfume wafted up from her skin and sent his senses spinning. "One hell of a doctor." His voice grew husky, as he alluded to the real reason for his toast. "One hell of a woman."

Long after the sun set, turning the turquoise ocean into a rippling silver ribbon, the pool outside the window drew vacationers who were reluctant to let the day slide into night.

Claire checked Orville's IV, his vital signs and draped a cover over Ruthie, who lay sleeping in a chaise not ten feet from her husband's bed.

Oh, to find that fierce, unselfish devotion in a mate, Claire reflected. Regretting what she'd missed, she closed Orville's door behind her and found Dugan lounging on the sitting room couch. He wore his new yellow shorts and the T-shirt that bore a likeness of the hotel set against the Caribbean.

She'd forgotten what great legs he had — fine, muscled thighs and hard calves. Only a hint of

148

the scars from his accident showed beneath the hem of his shorts. The T-shirt hugged the contours of his work-hardened chest and skimmed shoulders she'd once dug her fingernails into as she soared straight to heaven in Dugan's arms.

"How's Orville?" he asked.

"Sleeping."

"Think he'll make it?"

"If he behaves himself until we leave."

"You think he will?"

"I'm darned sure. He's scared half out of his wits."

"So is Ruthie," Dugan allowed.

"I know. She's in there sleeping in the chaise."

"Come over here and sit down," he said, patting the cushion beside him. "You deserve a rest."

"I — well . . ."

"I won't bite, Claire."

"Biting isn't what I'm worried about."

"Oh, no? Well, then there's something you ought to know about that dress you're wearing. About those bare shoulders." He cleared his throat. "They give me a few ideas that would make Dracula proud."

Trying not to think of Dugan's lips skimming her neck, Claire smoothed her hands over the swirly, gauzy skirt. "Lila bought this for me at the Mexican market."

"What do you say we hop a bus and go down there tomorrow afternoon after siesta time?"

"And shop?"

"Well, sure."

"I thought you hated to shop."

"I want you to have a good time. If that means shopping, I'm game. But tomorrow, I buy."

"The wire came through?"

"Uh-huh. In pesos, of course. I need a suitcase to haul the bills around."

"Who would have thought that we, that is, you and I . . ."

"Yeah, two former paupers, sitting here in the lap of luxury with a suitcase full of money."

"The money doesn't make me any happier. It's fun to spend, but it can't make up for . . . other things."

"Like?" he prodded her.

"A family. A home. Children."

Dugan picked up her hand and held it lightly on his knee. Her forearm brushed against the hard warmth of his thigh. Sitting there, hands linked, shoulder to shoulder on the couch, she could almost pretend he hadn't put an end to what she thought would endure forever.

God help her, thoughts of family still popped into her mind when she sat close to Dugan. She remembered the exquisite pleasure of learning their bold, athletic lovemaking had planted the seed of life in her. For three months they'd gloried in that knowledge. They'd talked about names, about outings they'd take when the baby came. They'd also spoken of siblings that would keep the baby company. Her vision clouded with the memories.

"What are you thinking about?" he asked.

"You don't want to know."

He nudged her with his shoulder. Without thinking, she tilted her head until it bumped against his. This was another instinctive gesture from the past. Dugan's hand slid up over her bare back and tangled in her hair.

She knew she should move, but she craved his touch, the soaring rush of blood that tingled her body. None of it made sense, especially when only a moment ago, she'd been thinking of the home and family she'd never had. But she was weary of fighting what had once been so wonderful.

"It was good for us, Claire, wasn't it?" Dugan brushed his lips across her cheek. Shuddering at the chill his gentle touch shot across her shoulders, she nodded.

"Couldn't we just think about the good times and work on making others?" he murmured into her ear.

"Here?"

"And at home."

"Home. You mean your place?"

"I can't think of a better place, can you?" he said, and his eyes shone a deep, warm brown.

"Whenever I go to the farm, I hurt, here—"

she pressed her hand over the cleavage of her dress "—so bad I have to leave."

"I wasn't aware you'd been out all that much."

"Several times actually. That first day, and when I checked your leg. When I'm there, I look at the wheat waving in the field, and I think of the day I lost Angela."

"I lost her, too, you know. When she died, so did a part of me. But please, let's not let those memories ruin tonight."

"What do you suggest?" she asked, turning to gaze fully into his eyes.

He grinned. The dimple poked deep into his cheek. "This."

In the span of a second, his hand secured her head in his open palm, and his mouth claimed her lips. Years might have passed, but lips and tongues, hands and arms knew precisely where to go and what to do. Claire and Dugan melded together in a full, open kiss, tongues tangling in the aftertaste of Burgundy wine and, yes, even pizza.

If Claire could have preserved one moment in time, she would have picked that kiss. No demands, no expectations cluttered the open honesty of their need, the hunger neither she nor Dugan attempted to hide. Neither spoke of pain or leavings. The only pain was that the kiss ended, and they were right back in that room with years and memories and shattered hearts to mend.

Dugan pressed his forehead against hers and licked his lips as if to memorize the taste of her. "I'm not sure I can talk."

"I thought you communicated quite eloquently just now."

"I want to say something in words, though."

"I almost wish you wouldn't, Dugan."

"I'm not giving up on us," he said and rubbed the tip of his nose across hers. "I want more than stolen kisses."

"In case you didn't notice, you didn't have to steal that kiss."

"Yeah, well, I want to capture more than just your lips, Claire. I want all of you and not for any brief Caribbean fling."

What had felt so natural for a few moments suddenly scared Claire to death. "I don't want to be captured. I don't want you making decisions for me. I don't want you assuming you can—"

"Shh," he told her. "I think I hear Orville."

Claire's shift ended at midnight when Lila arrived in nightgown, robe, and aqua plastic rollers.

"Okay, you two, out of here. My turn at the controls. Why don't you take in a disco or go for a stroll on the beach?"

"If I'm going to be any good to Orville, I need to get some sleep," Claire maintained with a healthy yawn.

Dugan stretched the kinks out of his shoulders. His thoughts snagged on one word, a thought, a promise.

Sleep. That meant they'd go back to the suite they shared. There they'd be alone for eight whole hours in a fancy hotel room.

Hmm.

"You asleep?"

Dugan's voice boomed across the pink marble floors and sent Claire ducking under the covers of the upstairs bedroom's king-sized bed.

She'd acquiesced when he'd insisted the women flip for the bedrooms while he flopped on the couch of the sitting room downstairs. Lila wanted the small bedroom next to the sitting room so she wouldn't have to negotiate the stairs every time she left. That left Claire all alone in the suite's massive bedroom.

For two hours she'd lain awake, imagining she could hear Dugan flip-flopping beneath her. She wished for footsteps on the winding wooden stairs. Yet she also dreaded them. Now that he was actually in her bedroom, a strange brand of terror gripped her heart. The darn thing clambered around in her chest like one of Dugan's frisky colts.

Thinking a little light might diffuse the tension, she crawled across the bed that seemed as big as all Texas and snapped on the lamp. A golden glow pooled on the polished walnut end table. She glanced around and sucked in a distinctly audible breath. Dugan stood in the doorway, wearing only a smile and the black swimsuit that looked a lot skimpier on his narrow hips than it had in the hotel boutique.

She pulled the sheet up over her breasts and decided to act nonchalant and adult about their shared accommodations. After all he was still standing in the doorway. He was wearing . . . something. The light from the lamp cast shadows into the hollows of Dugan's cheeks, into the dip between his pectorals. He still possessed a magnificent chest that gave her fingers a mind of their own.

Her gaze slid down over his flat abdomen and the narrow band of dark hair that descended into—wow! The thought of him strutting down the beach wearing only what hugged his body now conjured up possessive feelings she didn't know existed.

"I'm awake," she answered in a telltale, squeaky voice.

"Want to go for a swim?"

She glanced at the clock. "At three in the morning?"

"Might as well. Can't sleep."

"Well, give me time to slip into my suit."

"You can go like you are, Claire. I don't think anyone'd complain, least of all me."

She pitched a pillow across the room and instantly regretted it. With one hand Dugan grasped the flat pillow around the middle and chuckled. Even in the diffused light, she could see the glint of mischief in his dark, expressive eyes.

"So, you want to play, huh? Like old times?"

"Now, Dugan, I didn't mean to start . . ." She barely had time to duck. The pillow sailed across the room and struck the wall behind her with a muffled thud.

The fact she was only wearing a mid-thigh length T-shirt over purple bikini panties didn't faze her. This was war and she wasn't about to lose. While Dugan snatched a bath towel from the linen closet, she grabbed the other pillow and rolled off the mattress to hide in the shadows at the far side of the immense bed.

"Claire? Claire?" She heard the soft padding of his bare feet on the marble. He was getting closer. "Don't be a chicken. I know you're in here. I'll find you. You might as well come out now." He whipped the towel into a thick terry cord he snapped in the air.

From her hiding place, she snaked out her arm and snatched the towel from Dugan's unsuspecting hands. Then she delivered a downy blow to his backside. "Chicken, huh? How easily you forget!"

"Oh, we're going to play dirty, are we?" He dived across the bed and grabbed for her, barely snagging the tail of her cotton T-shirt as she tried to retreat. "Gotcha now!"

And so he did, with those bikini panties showing. In the old days she would have slipped out of the T-shirt to escape and led him on a merry chase around the room. If he'd cornered her, she would have disarmed him with feminine wiles. He'd always been a sucker for a saucy grin and bare breasts rubbing across his chest.

But these weren't the old days.

In a flash she retrieved the pillow at her side, smacked Dugan full in the face and scrambled like a hermit crab across the wide expanse of bed.

The laughter rumbled up from deep inside his chest, and in the blink of an eye twelve years hadn't passed. She was Claire, the new bride, and he, her oh-so-willing bridegroom. They were tussling on his grandfather's shaky bed, their young, firm muscles and their soaring hormones responding to the challenge.

"Still the little spitfire, huh? Well, I'll show you." Dugan rolled to his knees and lunged, nailing her calves and dragging her back across the bed. She could feel her T-shirt sliding up her bare chest and gasped when he flipped her over.

Dugan's hands stilled. All Claire could hear was his heavy breathing. All she could see was the hot glint of desire burning in his eyes. Kneeling now, he rocked back on his heels and rubbed

157

his palms up and down his thighs. "Ah, Claire, you're even more beautiful than before."

The air conditioning kicked on, cooling her heated skin and bringing a measure of sanity to her thoughts. She couldn't go back in time. They couldn't recapture what they'd lost. What could she have been thinking when she initiated such an encounter with Dugan?

With a shaking hand, she reached up to pull her T-shirt down over her breasts, but Dugan's hand stopped her.

"Don't. Please. Let me look at you." The muscles lining his strong, square jaw flexed. Before she could summon logic to respond to his entreaty, another spilled from his lips. "Let me touch you."

"Dugan, please . . ."

He hesitated, then murmured, "Do you mean no . . . or yes? If you mean no, I'll stop."

Logic said no. Her body screamed yes, this is what you've been wanting. As before, Dugan could read the wanting in her eyes and her hesitant posture. He could probably tell she'd rather leap off the balcony than tell him to leave her alone in that bed. There'd been so many nights alone when she'd dreamed of moments like this. When she'd curled around a hard knot of need in her abdomen—for one man. Only one. Dugan.

That man she so desperately wanted released

her hand. He sat there, kneeling on the bed, expelling a shaky breath.

So, reason had won out, and he'd relented. She guessed that was for the best. But why did the smart thing to do hurt so?

Dugan turned to move off the bed, then paused and looked back. A flicker of hope burned inside Claire. He gave her a lopsided smile, a shrug.

Not wanting to watch him leave, she closed her eyes and stifled an impending sob. She was still holding her breath when she felt his warm, moist lips on her navel. She sucked in her stomach muscles and trembled violently before cradling his head in her anxious hands and moaning. "Dugan . . . ah . . . oh."

"Claire, love, please don't hate me."

How could she hate him when his gently skimming fingers brought heaven to her breasts? When everywhere he touched he brought the pleasure she'd been so long denied? She had tried to go to bed with other men, but the results had been clinical. There would always be just one man for her—her first. Dugan.

"I don't hate you," she whispered. "I can't hate you."

"But you can't love me, hmm?" Dugan pulled her into his arms and rolled her to her side so she had to look into his eyes.

How could she think when the blood was thundering in her ears? When the swollen, male part of him pressed against her inner thigh?

"I . . . don't know," was all she'd say, for she couldn't let go of the past, no matter how delicious the feel of Dugan's arms.

"I could make love to you—right now—couldn't I?"

"You know you could. In a heartbeat."

"I'm not going to, Claire, much as I want to."

"Oh, Dugan. Then why did you do this to me?"

"I didn't do it. We did. And someday, when . . . if you find you can love me again, we'll finish what we've started. I don't want any regrets. Only our coming together, but it's got to be right and forever, or we'll both be sorry."

He was sending her away again and making decisions for her. Need flared to resentment. Resentment fired to anger that soared through her veins with an impulse to hurt back.

The pillow. Yes, the pillow.

She rolled out of Dugan's arms and to her knees. Grabbing the pillow that he'd flung at her from the doorway, she lifted it above her head and smacked him across the chest. "Why?" Another whop. "Why?" A third. "Why, why, why do you keep sending me away?"

All the hurt came pouring out from her heart and soul into that pillow. She must have whacked ten or twelve times. She didn't attempt to count. She only knew when the rage was over, the pillow had split and fluffy down feathers lay scattered across the bed. They clung to Dugan's chest and to the stubble of beard on his cheek.

Her arms fell limp to her side. For the first time in twelve years she was cleansed of anger and resentment.

Free.

Dugan said nothing, nor had he tried to defend himself during her assault.

No sooner had the anger abated than shame claimed its place. Claire lifted her palms to her face and wept.

Dugan pulled her back into his arms and smoothed his hands over her tangled hair. She cried into his chest until she could taste the salt of her own tears.

"Feel better?" he asked.

She sniffled loudly and nodded. "I-I'm sorry if I hurt you."

"Shh. No, you're not sorry. You did what you needed to do. I guess I deserved it."

"Will you forgive me?"

"I can't believe you asked such a stupid question. If you can forgive what I did to you—even though I did what I thought was right—how can I not overlook . . . a few goose feathers?"

"Did I hurt you?"

"Yeah, right."

She lifted her head and grinned at him. "Still Mr. Tough Guy, huh?"

"Isn't that why you married me?"

"I married you because you were good in bed."

"Why, Dr. Linwood, I can't believe you said such a thing."

"And I had a couple of other good reasons."

"Like?"

She sighed deeply against his chest. "Because I loved you, Dugan. I honestly, deeply loved you."

Only one corner of his mouth tipped up this time. Her careful selection of words hadn't escaped him. "Loved me. As in used to." He hugged her tight against his chest. "I swear, Claire. Someday I hope you can find it in your heart to apply that feeling to the present."

After a tender goodnight kiss, Dugan left Claire to get a couple of hours' sleep before her eight o'clock shift with Orville.

He hoped she slept better than he did.

He could easily have made love to Claire. Her glazed eyes told him she would have welcomed him into her body, and, God knows, he needed what she offered.

But he wanted more than sex. He didn't want a wild, rutting session like a stallion and a mare in heat. He wanted everything they'd had before . . . and more.

He wanted Claire to return his love, not just his passion. He needed to hear her say the words.

He was shaving in the downstairs bathroom when Lila banged into the room whistling. He gave her a quick peck on the cheek and heard her feet plunking up the stairs. A few moments later he glanced up to find her staring at him in the mirror, a smile playing at her lips.

"What in the world happened upstairs last night?" she asked.

"Claire and I, we . . . uh . . . got into a little . . . that is, we had a pillow —"

"Fight." She clasped her hands beneath her chin and grinned. "What fun!"

"I guess you could call it fun. But before you get any ideas, that's all it was. I slept down here."

"Sleepin' wasn't what I was thinkin' about," she said coyly.

"There wasn't any of that either," he tossed over his shoulder, "unfortunately."

"Well, don't give up on the girl."

"Believe me, I have no intention of doing such a thing."

"What're you two plannin' after Claire's shift?"

"Depends on how Orville's doing."

"That old windbag's fine. He did have a bit of flutter in his heart last night, but nothing much else."

"You still think we'll be able to leave day after tomorrow?"

"Claire says so."

Dugan toweled off the excess shaving cream from his face. "I hate to leave, in a way. I need to get back to the ranch and all, but, well, some good things have happened here."

Lila stood there for an uncomfortable moment, staring at Dugan in the mirror, tapping her lip with her forefinger. What was the woman scheming?

"Am I right in assumin' your feelings for Claire are a bit more than friendly?"

Chuckling, he said, "You assume right. I'm not sure it's going to do me any good, though. I hurt her a lot. She's trying, but I'm not sure she can forgive me, or forget."

"You'd better not go and break that girl's heart again," Lila warned him.

"I can promise you, I won't do that."

"Hmm. Well, then, here's the plan. Tomorrow after Claire's morning shift ends at eight, I want you two to take off, go where you want. I'll work the eight to four and the four to twelve. That'll give you a whole day to soak up the sun, lie on the beach, go snorkeling, do—" she winked "—whatever you please."

She'd put a whole lot of emphasis on the "whatever," Dugan noted, so he guessed she hadn't been fooled a bit by his lily white story about the pillow fight. "I'm not sure Claire'll agree to leave Orville that long."

"Nonsense. If he's only restin', he'll be fine. Besides, she'll have her beeper."

Lila's eyes sparkled. A foxy grin crept over her face. "I want you two to have all the time you need to . . . sightsee."

* * *

Claire fell asleep under an umbrella on the beach that afternoon. She'd taken only two sips of the giant margarita Dugan ordered for her from the hotel waiter who worked the narrow, sandy stretch.

The need to please her, to do something—anything—to see her smile like she'd smiled at him last night was about to overwhelm him. Yet a niggling doubt was eating away at his new line of positive thinking.

Claire, he had noticed, had slipped easily into the good life Cancún offered. He wondered if she'd ever settle for being his farming, ranching wife again. There in the windswept, rolling hills of West Texas, the sun rose each day on a whole new list of chores. While he would never—ever—permit Claire to labor in the fields again, life on the stretch of sandy loam east of town would never be what he'd call cushy.

He frowned at the thought of the two-story house she was building in town. A new set of insecurities clouded his mind. Living in that house, she'd be close to the majority of patients in her practice. That's where she needed to live, he admitted, not ten miles and a bumpy twenty-minute ride into town on a road that became impassible with sudden rains.

Which left him and his acres of crops and cattle and horses where?

165

That afternoon his worries grew while he watched Claire poke around a mini-mall of shops full of expensive stuff women loved. He watched her try on a gleaming silver ring set with amethysts. She angled it to reflect the overhead lights, then reluctantly handed it back to the jeweler. Dugan gladly shelled out two hundred and fifty bucks so she could have that ring, a bargain at that price.

Fine things for a fine woman made sense, especially when he had the cash to spend and didn't have to charge the purchase. But he would've been a fool to overlook Claire's taste for the extravagant.

He'd worked hard to make his ranch pay. Still, there would be slim years when he'd have to watch every nickel spent, with or without Claire's income to supplement his. Could she bear up under such intense scrutiny?

He'd suggested they ride the bus to the mall for fifty cents apiece. Claire had opted for a cab at seven bucks. She reasoned she didn't have enough time or energy to waste on taking the bus. That made perfectly good sense to Dugan. God knows she deserved the pampering. But darned if it didn't seem like she was trying to make up for all the sacrifices of a lifetime in one fell swoop.

He worried Claire would stumble into that pit of debt that had been his granddaddy's undoing—and theirs. After Claire had almost died delivering Angela, he'd sworn he'd never owe another man a penny. Claire, on the other hand, was charging like there was no tomorrow.

Whatever he thought about her spending habits, he decided nothing would be too good for her on their last day. He had a wad of pesos left, even after he'd paid the hotel bill in advance while she tended to Orville.

He planned to spend every single one on Claire. By doing so, he hoped they'd make new memories to replace the old, painful ones.

Claire wasted no time changing into a vibrant aqua T-shirt and matching shorts for their last day in Cancún. She smiled at Dugan over a platter of fresh fruit and those yummy pastries at the Palacio's cafe on the beach.

He hadn't complained about the new blue shorts and shirt she'd bought him at the hotel boutique that morning. With his deep tan and warm, brown eyes, he looked good enough to gobble up with the pastry.

"What do you say we grab a cab and drive over to see the ruins in Tulum?" she suggested.

"A taxi, huh?" he said and gazed out over the softly rolling surf. "How long a drive do you figure it is?"

"That's the good part about a taxi—only an hour and a half. The bus is bound to be pokier. We can take a quick look around, then leave, without waiting for everyone on the bus to get their fill."

Dugan took her hand and ran his thumb over the silver and amethyst ring he'd bought her. He'd give anything to slip a diamond on the other hand. Years ago all he'd been able to afford was an imitation gold band that had fallen apart. She'd patched up what was left with electrical tape and worn it proudly.

"Taking a cab — would that make you happy?" he asked.

"Yes!"

"I'll go arrange it then."

"Oh, Dugan, thanks!" She threw her arms around his neck and gave him a big hug that set his heart to thumping.

Maybe riding through the jungle in the privacy of a cab wouldn't be such a bad idea after all.

Tulum was seventy-eight miles south of Cancún on a narrow road that made the one that skirted Dugan's ranch look like an interstate.

Arm in arm with Dugan, Claire stood atop *el castillo,* a forty-foot pyramid-shaped tower that looked out over the glistening Caribbean waters.

"Mom and Dad used to talk about coming here. They were archeology freaks. By way of books, at least. I don't think they ever got outside Texas. I wish they could have seen this beautiful place."

"Why didn't they travel?"

"They were always living for tomorrow, never

for today. Like you and me, Dugan. That's what we did. We lived for tomorrow and lost sight of today."

"Until there wasn't any today."

"Or tomorrow," she glumly added. She turned to him and felt the urge to explain her newfound philosophy of life.

"That's why I'm not going to hoard my money. I'm going to spend it. I want to travel and see things and meet people. I might as well." She shrugged at a fact she'd come to accept. "I'll never have kids to save for."

"But what about emergencies?"

"I'm not a fool. I'll put some money by."

Returning his gaze to the ocean, Dugan didn't express his disapproval, but he didn't have to. She could read it in his tightly compressed lips.

"You've worked hard making your ranch a success. Don't you want to cut loose and indulge yourself before you're too old or ill, like Orville?"

"Orville's that sick?"

"I can't be sure until we get him to a hospital for some tests, but he may need surgery. He's how old?"

"Seventy-five, six, something like that."

"Seventy-six. Not ancient, but heart surgery's not easy to recover from. I wouldn't want to be in his place and not have seen Cancún and Europe and maybe even Japan."

"You're serious about seeing all those places?"

"Sure. Aren't you?"

"I'll tell you what, Doc," he said, and she started at his use of the title again. "I'm happy being right where I am in Sierra. Every day I wake up, and I see the sun rise. The air's clean. I've got all I need and a whole lot more. I could stay right there the rest of my life and be happy. That is, if I had the right company."

The right company.

Dugan gave her a questioning look. She knew he was searching for even a hint of reassurance that she might be "the right company."

But truth to tell, she wasn't sure she'd ever be.

Chapter Eight

The day wasn't turning out the way Dugan had planned. Not by a long shot.

He and Claire rode back to the hotel from the Mayan ruins in the open-windowed cab where he'd thought they'd snuggle, talk, and do what other delicious things their bodies dictated.

Instead, a wide swatch of cracking vinyl stretched between them, as he gazed out one window, Claire, the other. A silence hung between them as heavy as the steamy jungle humidity.

Dugan was almost glad when the taxi pulled into the hotel, and he shelled out a wad of pesos.

After showering—separately, to Dugan's continuing dismay—they lunched on the beach and took a double parasail ride over the ocean.

They floated over the Caribbean like birds on a foil, removed from all sound except an occasional snap of the chute's silk. Somehow the atmosphere was just right for Dugan to ponder Claire's attitudes about life and money and travel.

Her parents had died in their forties, never investing in anything but their modest home and their lovely daughter. Understandably, Claire wanted more from life than the sacrifices they had made for a security that, in a way, became their prison. Dugan hoped she realized, though, that no amount of money could buy things of true value — especially love.

Still, he planned one hell of an evening, and hang the cost.

They dined at an intimate Italian restaurant recommended by the hotel's concierge. Waiters hovered over them and brought dish after dish of mouth-watering food, half of which Dugan had never tasted before.

Next he took Claire to a chic disco called Daddy-O's with a laser light show that made her face glow like an enchanted child's. Encouraged by the improvement in her mood, he whisked her out on the dance floor. They delighted the crowd with a whirling, twirling version of the Texas two-step.

The cab they took back to the hotel screeched to a halt at the top of the brick circle drive.

"How about a walk on the beach?" Dugan

asked as the doorman opened the cab for Claire, glancing admiringly at the bare back her black dress revealed.

"I'd like that." She looked down at her watch and announced regretfully, "I can't believe it. Only one more hour, and I turn into a pumpkin."

One more hour to work magic, he thought and prayed for a miracle.

They strolled through the almost deserted hotel lobby, then meandered along paths skirting the pool, the swim-up bar, and the beachwear boutique. The sand grated beneath their feet as they descended the stairs to the beach and drew deep, refreshing breaths of the salty air.

By unspoken consent, Claire and Dugan stepped onto the beach and paused to watch and listen, hands linked.

Claire was vaguely aware of sand seeping through the open spaces of her cocktail sandals. She didn't care. She wanted to remember the beach — the sights, the sounds, the smells, the satiny feel of her skin and Dugan's in the humid air — exactly as it was this last night together.

The foam of the waves gleamed white in the moonlight as the ocean flung itself at the Caribbean shore. The surf receded, snatching back with its powerful undertow, the shells and ocean critters it had discarded on the deserted, pristine beach only a moment before.

The earth giveth. The earth taketh away, Claire thought with regret.

While Dugan steadied her, holding her hand firmly, she slipped out of her black sandal heels and slung them over her shoulder on a finger. His hand was warm, the callouses softened by four days' absence from the demands of manual labor. When they flew back home, he would resume his farming-ranching chores, and she would devote herself to her practice.

"I'm going to miss being with you when we get back," Dugan said.

"Funny. That's just what I was thinking."

"After this place, will you settle for going back to plain old Sierra?"

She laughed softly, but the roar of the sea gobbled up the sound. "Of course. I've called every day to check on my patients . . . especially Pamela Sue."

"She's almost due, isn't she?"

"Five weeks, if she has her dates right."

"Everything normal so far?"

"So far."

"Good. What's she going to do with the baby when it's born?"

"Keep it, I think."

"Can she support a kid and herself?"

"That's questionable. I'll try to help her, but I can only do so much."

"I'm sorry," Dugan said, shaking his head.

"For what?"

He paused, his expression grave, his tone serious. "I'm sorry as hell you can't have any more babies."

"Now, Dugan, you know that isn't your fault."

"If you hadn't married me, you'd probably have a houseful of kids right now."

"Maybe I would. Maybe I wouldn't. I could make myself sick if I thought about everything I was going to miss because of some quirk of fate." She squeezed his hand consolingly. "Every time someone in Sierra has a baby, I'll get to examine the little tyke and watch it grow."

"Not the same as having your own."

"Please, Dugan. I've accepted the fact I can't have children." But suddenly Claire wondered if that shortcoming bothered him more than he'd let on. "Let's not ruin tonight with what could have been."

She plunked her shoes into the sand and sat beside them, gazing out over the dark, rolling waves. Dugan hesitated, then joined her, propping his forearms on bent knees.

He'd worn the white pants and embroidered shirt she'd bought him. He took her hand in his and propped it on his thigh. A simple, casual gesture, but Dugan's skin burned hot through the soft cotton, as if he were running a fever.

The wanting rolled up inside her, as powerful as the ocean's undertow. She wished she could make love to Dugan. However, he wouldn't accept less than a full confession of love, and, she guessed, a commitment to bind them together for eternity.

She wasn't sure she could ever make that promise again.

He squeezed her hand and traced the ring finger of her left hand with his forefinger. "I love you, Claire. You know that, don't you?"

"I . . . Dugan, I don't know what to say."

"Don't say anything. Just listen. I never stopped loving you. I know you thought I did. I know you thought I didn't care if you lived until tomorrow. But all that was a smoke screen to help you."

"Dugan—"

"I was wrong. I'll admit that now. And I'm all torn up inside thinking about you and me. I love you, sure, but I don't know if I could live with you."

"Live with me?" Dugan's words stung Claire's ears with their unexpected negative connotation.

"You're different now. Maybe I am, too. I'm content sticking around the ranch. You want to see the world. I pinch the nickel until the buffalo—"

"Roars," Claire provided, grinning wryly.

"You like to spend your money. Maybe," he said, turning her face with a finger beneath her chin, "you're right. Maybe it is too late for us."

They gazed into each other's eyes, saying nothing more, only hurting. Claire was afraid the burning lump in her throat might choke her. In the past few days she'd finally released the past and all the hurt. She wanted Dugan as her husband again. But just when she thought they'd banished all the ghosts that had kept them apart, new problems had emerged for them to face, new pains to endure.

Would the suffering never end for them?

"Come here, pretty lady," he said, tugging her hand. "I swear, tonight I almost decked a few guys gawking at you in that dress."

She'd delighted at the gleam in Dugan's eyes when she'd descended the stairs into the sitting room and twirled before him for his approval.

He pulled her across his lap and snuggled her back to his chest. Though she felt cared for and protected, that wasn't what she wanted at that moment. She wanted to feel Dugan touch her. She pulled his hand to her abdomen and sighed. She wanted to finish what they'd started last night.

Dugan's hand moved to her breast, his lips to the curve of her neck. "Ah, Claire. You smell like those wildflowers in Joseph's pasture, and—" he bent to kiss a lower spot on her neck "—you taste like dessert."

She laughed. "Dessert? How romantic!"

Suddenly his hands grasped her waist and turned her to face him. She sat astride him, that wanting part of her pressed over the bulge of him there. She laced her arms around his neck and felt his hands slide over her bare back.

"You are my dessert, Claire. See?"

He angled his head, fitted his lips over hers, and tangled his tongue in her anxious mouth. Claire poured herself into the kiss as if she might never have a chance for another. Tonight Dugan was hers, and she was his.

And tomorrow? She didn't want to think about it.

The cold reality of tomorrow struck at 6:00 a.m. Claire, Lila, and Dugan scurried about the Garrisons' suite, cramming souvenirs, medical equipment, and medications into already bursting suitcases.

They waited until the last minute to move Orville into the wheelchair Claire had paid the bellhop a small fortune to scrounge up and deliver to the room.

In preparation for the trip, Claire had gradually increased Orville's exercises so he could endure the transfer to the plane and the excitement of the flight. Still, she worried about his condition. When he was safely tucked away in his hospital bed in Lubbock, she would breathe easier.

During the flight Lila gladly kept a fairly grumpy Dugan company. She sat in the copilot's seat and chatted non-stop. Claire and

Ruthie fussed over Orville in the plane's passenger section, which Dugan had customized as an air ambulance.

As Dugan revved up the plane's engines, Claire glanced out the window and bid a melancholy, regretful good-bye to paradise—and the happiest four days of her life.

"Looks like you had a better time than we did," Orville told her.

"Yes, I suppose we—that is, I—did."

"Things any better between you two?" Orville asked, tipping his head at the pilot's seat.

"A little."

"Only a little?"

"Uh-huh. And that's stretching it."

"A little's better than nothing. I'd like to think what happened to this old heart helped yours and Dugan's."

"Playing cupid, are you?" she teased him while she checked the flow of oxygen.

"Wouldn't take much, the way I see it."

She patted his hand and gave him an encouraging smile. How she wished she could tell Orville—herself, for that matter—that the four days in Cancún had solved all their problems. "At least we're friends now."

"Friends? Who said anything about friends? I was thinking more along the lines of—"

"Orville, leave the poor girl alone," Ruthie insisted. "All a person has to do is look in her eyes to tell she's hurting."

Oh, dear, Claire thought. If she was that transparent, there'd be hell to pay once she returned to Sierra.

After a delay in Brownsville while the U.S. Customs officials searched every bag they'd brought back from Mexico, Dugan flew straight to Lubbock.

Before they left the hotel, Claire had phoned a cardiologist in Lubbock, who'd preadmitted Orville to the hospital. An ambulance awaited them at the airport and whisked the Garrisons off to the hospital. Claire and Dugan followed in a cab. They stayed long enough to make sure Orville's admission to the hospital went smoothly and for Claire to consult with his cardiologist.

An hour later Dugan breezed onto the runway on his ranch, and Cinderella's coach turned into a pumpkin.

In his absence all hell had broken loose on the farm. A violent wind storm had blown the roof off his livestock barn. Panicked by the blinding wind and rain, six feeder cattle had broken through the pasture fence and trampled a bunch of Joseph Witcomb's sweet potatoes.

Obviously distracted by the work cut out for him, Dugan loaded Claire's suitcase and medical equipment into his foreman's pickup and bid her a quick farewell.

The next seven days dragged by. Claire didn't see Dugan once. She didn't realize how this was wearing on her until Pamela Sue made a perceptive comment during her routine prenatal visit to the clinic.

"You don't seem the same since you got back," the teenager observed as she lay on the examining table.

"Neither do you, my dear."

Claire wondered just how much showed in her eyes and her facial expressions. Could Pamela Sue tell that every time the phone rang, she prayed the caller would be Dugan? Did she have any idea how much she missed the husky tenor of his voice? The touch of his hand?

"You're positively glowing," she told Pamela Sue.

"Glowing and growing. I think I'm about to pop."

"Pretty good description," Claire said with a chuckle. "You can get dressed now."

"Is my baby okay?"

"From what I can tell, healthy as a horse."

"Maybe that's what I'm going to have." She smoothed her hands over her protruding belly, then braced the small of her back with her hand. "My back is killing me."

"Are you doing your exercises?" Claire asked.

"Every day. Lila bugs me till I do."

"Good for her. I want you to let me know the first sign of labor. We'll drive you into Lubbock. I've made arrangements to deliver the baby at the hospital."

"What if there isn't time?" the girl asked with wide, fearful eyes.

"First babies usually take quite a while. I really don't think you have anything to worry about," Claire reassured her. "And remember, I have my beeper. You call me, and I'll drop everything and run."

Now dressed in one of the cheerful maternity outfits Claire and Lila had bought her, Pamela Sue turned her back to leave. Her shoulders trembled. Claire heard a poorly stifled sob.

She turned Pamela Sue to face her. Her heart went out to the mother-to-be who was still such a child herself. "What's the matter, sweetheart? Last minute jitters?"

She shook her head of fiery curls. Tears cascaded over her smooth, freckled cheeks. "Lila says she'll be there to help me."

"But?"

"I just wish . . . oh, never mind."

"You can talk to me. What is it?"

She bit her lip and looked at the ceiling as if to control her emotions. How young Pamela Sue was to have to face her adult situation.

"I just wish this baby had a daddy. Someone kind and gentle who would hold it and love it and support it . . . and me. Someone who would change its diapers and feed it a bottle and teach it its ABCs. Someone like . . . your

Dugan."

"My Dugan?" That observation nearly knocked the breath out of Claire. He wasn't hers, except perhaps in the futile yearnings of her heart.

Pamela Sue nodded. "The boy who—the real daddy of my baby—slammed the phone in my ear when I told him. No, that's not right. First he told me to get lost. No way was he marrying me or supporting no kid."

Claire slid her arm around the teenager's shoulders and gave her the hug she desperately needed. "If only other girls your age could hear your story. Maybe they'd wait . . . or be more careful."

"You won't be finding me in this condition again, Dr. Linwood. I promise you that. I don't know how I'm going to do it just yet, but I'm going to make something of myself. Like you."

"That a girl," Claire said and gave Pamela Sue her brightest smile. But inside she was crying. Sure she had made something of herself, but she'd never know the joy of raising her own child.

She noted Pamela Sue's weight gain and vital signs in her file and almost fell off her stool when the girl asked, "You want kids someday?"

Claire closed the manila file, her patient's innocent question casting despair over her lonely body. She didn't want to relate the story of Angela's birth and subsequent death to Pamela

Sue. At the moment she was functioning as a doctor. The emotions that would surely tumble out with the telling might frighten the young and impressionable patient. Yet, she wasn't one to lie, and Pamela Sue was sizing up the uncomfortable silence with a curious eye.

"Did I ask a touchy question, Dr. Linwood?"

Claire tidied up the work area with feigned nonchalance. "It's all right. On your way out, be sure to make an appointment for next week."

"Don't you want children?" Pamela Sue asked softly.

"Oh, my." Claire paused, then quietly added, "Of course I do."

"Then, why—"

"Did your question upset me?"

"Yes."

"I didn't want to tell you this, because I don't want you to be concerned about your baby, but I had a baby, Pamela Sue. Her name was . . . Angela."

"Where is she now?"

Claire drew a deep breath to steady herself. "She died."

"Oh, Dr. Linwood! I'm so sorry! I mean, nobody told me."

"I don't want you to worry about your baby. The circumstances aren't anything like mine. There wasn't a doctor. There were complications. I-I want children, Pamela Sue, but, well . . . I can't have any more."

Two young arms flung around Claire's neck. Claire felt odd being comforted by a young woman whose needs were so much greater than her own. Still Pamela Sue's concern and affection touched her—and helped soothe her aching heart.

"Was the baby Dugan's?"

Claire sighed deeply. "Yes."

"I heard you was married."

"Yes, a long time ago."

"Must have been awful for both of you, losing a baby and all."

"Yes, it was awful." Claire patted the girl's back and smiled into her eyes. "We survived, though. Life goes on."

"Is that why you didn't want to be married to him anymore?"

"Who said I didn't want to be married to him anymore?"

Pamela Sue shrugged. "People talk."

"Well, I'll tell you what," Claire went on, deciding she could at least set this sweet, questioning girl straight. "I didn't give up on him. He gave up on me. And, yes, losing Angela put a tremendous strain on our marriage."

"He still loves you."

"H-how do you know that?" Claire stammered.

"Easy. All you have to do is watch him when you're around. He can't look at anyone but you."

"I'm afraid you're an incurable romantic."

"If I am, so's half the town."

"Well, half the town'd better learn I didn't come back to marry Dugan again."

"They don't think that!"

"I honestly don't care if they do. All I know is, Dugan and I are . . ." she searched for the precise words he'd used that last night on the beach. ". . . different people now. It just won't work for us."

"Maybe not, Dr. Linwood, but I'll tell you what. If it was me standing in your place, I'd bust my skinny rear end trying."

They had no sooner opened the door than Claire's duty nurse bustled down the hallway, her eyes wide, her face flushed, her hands clenched tightly.

"Dr. Linwood, I've got to talk to you. Quick."

"What is it?"

"An emergency."

"Who?" Claire asked.

"Gunther Boone."

"Where is he?"

"In that cabin of his out in the country."

"Is his emphysema acting up?"

"You guessed it. He could hardly talk when he called for all the coughing."

"Get him on the phone," Claire said, heading back toward her office. She wondered if Gunther had any oxygen in that cabin of his. If

186

he'd only come to see her, she could have arranged for the delivery of a supply.

"I can't. He coughed so hard he dropped the phone. I yelled and I yelled, but he didn't answer. He just kept coughing."

"I'd better get right out then," Claire said, stuffing her stethoscope into her medical bag. "I've never been to his place. Could you jot down the directions while I load some supplies into the car?"

"Sure thing."

Claire took off down the hall. A half dozen steps later she ran full force into a massive wall of chest.

"Dugan."

"Hi, Doc. Where's the fire?"

Claire rubbed her forehead where she'd smacked into Dugan's chin. She told herself she had to ignore the tingles of feeling absolutely alive now that she'd set eyes on him after seven long days—and nights.

"No fire. I've got a house call to make. A cabin call, that is. Gunther."

Dugan narrowed his gaze. "I don't like the idea of you going out there alone."

"Well, I'm going. The man's sick. He needs me. From the way I hear he was coughing, I doubt he'll feel like being rude and obnoxious this time."

"His cabin isn't easy to find. I know the way. I'll take you."

187

"Oh, would you?" Claire said with a sigh of relief. "Every minute counts."

"We'll drive your car. If you need to bring him into the clinic, he'll be more comfortable in the Lincoln than my pickup."

He turned to Pamela Sue. "Could you find someone to drive my pickup out to the ranch?" He handed her the keys. "My foreman's waiting for the load of vaccines in the cab. We just got word there's been an outbreak of blackleg in the county where I bought my new calves. They've got to be inoculated before he goes to Lubbock to pick up his fiancé."

"Sure," the girl responded. "I'll call over to Imogene's. Don't you worry." She smiled first at him, then at Claire, her gaze darting briefly to Dugan's hand still protectively curled around Claire's arm. "I'll find someone to drive it out. You two get out of here now. And if you finish up early enough, why don't you take in the church social tonight." She rested her chin on tented fingers. "It is Friday night, you know."

While Claire braced herself for what they might find in Gunther's cabin, Dugan barreled down the dirt road past his farm a couple of miles. Then he steered the Lincoln on a zigzag path over rutted dirt roads before he braked in a cloud of sand and dust.

Gunther's no-frills log cabin was tucked into

a dip in the eroded range and ringed by mesquite trees and sagebrush. It gave Claire the eerie feeling of another day and time. Abraham Lincoln's to be precise. Maybe back then someone had nurtured from the sandy loam soil the hardwood trees needed to build the rustic cabin.

A chimney poked through the tattered asphalt shingle roof. Scrub wood stacked against one wall told Claire that Gunther depended on nature's bounty for heat. Beneath a makeshift carport on one side of the cabin stood the 1952 DeSoto that Gunther kept in a semblance of running order.

As she grabbed her bag and opened the car's door, the only sounds that greeted Claire were the scolding cry of a blue jay, the crow of a rooster, and a rattling cough that drifted from the confines of the cabin through an open window.

At least Gunther was still alive.

To describe the cabin's interior as austere was a vast understatement. The only furniture in the living room was a massive couch upholstered in dingy sixties-vintage plaid Herculon. That plus a wooden door propped on concrete blocks that apparently served as Gunther's coffee table.

A quick glance into the kitchen revealed a card table and one folding chair. Pantry shelves along one wall were tidily stocked with dozens of cans of beef stew, soup, and canned milk, all of generic brand. A telltale yellow stained the cabin windows. The smell of cigarette smoke pervaded the air.

"The bedroom's that way," Dugan said, nodding his head, but he didn't have to tell Claire. She followed the coughing into a darkened room. There she found Gunther propped up against the wall in his rusting iron bed. Even though the warmth of late summer still lingered in the October air, he was dressed in long handles and sat with a pillow pressed against his chest.

"Gunther. Hi. Dr. Linwood. You don't sound so good."

"About time," he managed to force out. His face was red and his hands clutched a white cloth stained with blood-tinged mucous.

Claire rolled up a blind to provide the light she needed for her examination. "How long have you been spitting up that blood?"

"A . . . c-couple of . . . w-weeks," he answered between coughs.

Poor Gunther was literally drowning in the fluids filling the air sacs of his lungs. By now they probably resembled soaked sponges more than life-sustaining organs. Claire couldn't stop the disease's progression, but she also couldn't leave him to waste away alone out there.

Sierra was blessed with a late-arriving winter. However, by Thanksgiving, in seven weeks, Gunther wouldn't be able to tolerate the crisp nights and mornings.

Her only hope was to move him to the medical complex in Lubbock where she'd heard a study into the advanced stages of emphysema was about to begin. The researchers would make Gunther as comfortable as possible, most likely without charge.

She stubbed out a cigarette still smoking in a glass motel ash tray at Gunther's bedside.

The researchers would make darned sure Gunther couldn't get his hands on any cigarettes, she thought, shaking her head.

"The blood isn't a good sign, Gunther," Claire told him as she listened to his lungs. "There isn't much I can do for you at this point. Your best hope is to let Dugan fly you into Lubbock to the medical center."

Gunther shook his head violently, managing to whisper in a strained voice, "I don't have no money, Doc."

"I'll make a couple of calls before we leave. There's every possibility you can be worked into a study they're doing at the medical center. It shouldn't cost you a cent."

Surprise flickered across his wrinkled brow, which soon furrowed into a deep frown. "I still can't afford no trip in no airplane."

"Don't worry about the money," she told him, understanding only too well his dismal financial situation. "The important thing is to get you there as soon as possible."

191

"If you'll tell me where your clothes are," Dugan said from the doorway, "I'll give you a hand getting dressed."

"I ain't goin' nowhere," Gunther announced stubbornly and Claire noted that his current coughing fit had subsided.

"Gunther, please. You called me for help. I'm prescribing what's best for you. I just wish you'd come to see me when I opened the clinic. That wouldn't have cost you a dime."

"You would have done what you're doing now. Put me in a damned hospital. Then I couldn't have earned no money."

"Some things are more important than money, Gunther. Your health, for one."

"Easy for you to say, being a rich doctor from the big city."

"Now Gunther—"

"I can't go to no hospital. I got my jobs, Doc," he pleaded. "What about my jobs?"

"You aren't in any condition to work. You're going, and that's that. I'll call the hospital and arrange your preadmission."

Gunther either ran out of arguments or the strength to complain. Dugan moved to a closet and pulled a red plaid shirt off a hanger. While watching him help Gunther slip his arms into the sleeves, Claire noticed Dugan frowning at the wall behind the bed.

"What's wrong?" Claire asked.

Dugan didn't answer her. He left the patient

to button his shirt while he poked at something lodged between two logs of the wall. With a little persistence, he plucked what looked like a piece of green fabric from the seam. He unrolled it.

"What is it?" Claire asked. "A cigarette?"

"Nope. A twenty-dollar bill," Dugan answered, studying the wall's seams more closely. "And if I don't miss my guess, every wall in this room is chock full of them."

Claire's gaze shot to the seams between the logs. "If all those rolls are twenties, Gunther could have more money than both of us."

Gunther glared up at both of them. "So what?"

"So how long have you been squirreling your money away like this?" Dugan asked.

"Long as I can remember. You got somethin' against savin'?"

"I do when a man needs the money for his health. Gunther, why didn't you see a doctor years ago? You've obviously had the money."

"Money's for savin', not spendin'."

"Who said?" Dugan demanded.

"My daddy. He lost most everything in the Depression. Everything except this here cabin."

Claire listened to the exchange between the two men, the futility of her mission weighing heavily on her. If only Gunther had spent a few of his precious dollars when his coughing began, she might not be staring at a dying man.

In Philadelphia she'd watched a patient in his sixties die in agony from the same ailment as Gunther's. She couldn't undo the abuse he'd heaped on his body anymore than she could make Gunther's diseased lungs healthy again. But she could help him make his last months as comfortable as possible.

"You've worked hard for your money, Gunther, haven't you?" Claire said softly.

"Durned right."

"You never married?"

"Nope."

"Do you have any relatives?"

"It's no secret I don't."

Claire felt immediate sympathy for the man. She knew only too well the meaning of loneliness. "Then you don't have anyone to worry about but yourself."

This time he merely nodded.

"And you're an intelligent man."

Gunther's chin shot up a fraction. "Like to think so."

"Then forget what happened to your daddy, rest his soul." Her gaze veered briefly to Dugan. She wanted to scream, you listen to this, too. "You've got to think of yourself now. What'll make you happy. What'll make you comfortable. No more worry about a Depression."

She hesitated, weighing the wisdom of being direct in her admonition, then deciding directness was probably all Gunther understood. "Because if you don't get yourself to a hospital soon, you won't live long enough to worry about any Depression."

Gunther relented and agreed to check into the hospital. But he absolutely refused to fly, citing every excuse but the real one—his obvious fear of flying.

Since he had stabilized, Claire figured he could handle the hour-and-a-half car ride into Lubbock. She made the necessary calls to arrange his admission. Dugan remembered his foreman had a date that night with his fiancé in Lubbock. He phoned him with a request.

The kindly foreman agreed to meet them on the highway and drive Gunther to the Lubbock hospital. There a lung specialist affiliated with the emphysema research project would examine Gunther as a candidate for the program.

Dugan promised to personally empty the cabin walls of the bills Gunther had squirreled away. He would deposit them in a savings account at Sierra's bank, an account Gunther could draw on by a simple phone call to Orville.

"You think you got through to him?" Dugan asked as he steered Claire's Lincoln back down the dirt road toward his ranch.

Did I get through to you? she wanted to ask. *Do you understand why focusing on money too intensely can be hazardous to your health? To your happiness?* But she didn't feel like a confrontation with another stubborn male whose thinking had been warped by a relative's misfortune.

The day had been long, her schedule demanding. The muscles in the small of her back clenched and released in a painful pattern. If she initiated an argument with Dugan, she might slip and say something she regretted. For their last few minutes together, she wanted to simply enjoy his company. Fantasize about what it would be like if they were driving to their ranch, not his.

"At least he agreed to go to the hospital," Claire said.

Dugan turned left off the road and bumped over the grate. "Never thought I'd see the day. Hey, look. The truck's here. I wonder who Pamela Sue found to drive it out."

"Any new dents?"

Dugan frowned. "Not that I can tell. Why?"

"Then you can be sure it wasn't Lila."

Dugan chuckled. "Why don't you step inside for a spell. I still make a mean cup of coffee. Afterward, we could take in that church social, if you like."

Do you still work magic on a back? Claire wondered. Oh, for the exquisite pleasure of his hands on her body. Kneading away the tension in the small of her back, then inching up her spine with firm, massaging fingers to work out the kinks in her shoulders and neck.

"I really should be getting back," she told him.

"What's the rush?"

"I have some paperwork to do," was all she could think to say.

He merely shrugged and gave up on his pursuit more easily than Claire would have preferred.

She watched him saunter around the front of her car to open the passenger door for her. He'd always be a gentleman, good times or bad. In Philadelphia she'd found no one like him, no one who came close to the self-confident male who could turn her insides to jelly with a smile, a wink, a memory.

His hand on the door, he hesitated, tipping his cowboy hat back. "Say, Doc. You wouldn't be trying to avoid me, would you?"

"If I'd been trying to, I wouldn't have let you drive me to Gunther's."

"Then you won't mind stepping inside for a spell."

Said the spider to the fly. "A cup of coffee does sound good," she relented.

Claire hadn't been in Dugan's house since the last time she'd checked the wounds on his leg. Then his housekeeper had been posted at her side to diffuse the spiraling attraction between them.

How would she and Dugan react to being alone — really alone — for the first time since that night on the beach in Cancún?

If he shared her nervousness, he didn't show it. He pushed open the front door and stood aside to let her enter first. "Why don't you go get comfy on the couch? I'll be back quick as a whistle with that coffee."

Claire glanced across the room and grabbed Dugan's arm. "Oh, my God, Dugan. Look!"

Chapter Nine

"Pamela Sue! What happened?" Dugan asked as Claire hurried to the girl's side.

The child-mother sat, legs crossed yoga-style, in his harvest gold recliner angled before the stone fireplace. Her eyes were squeezed tight, tears streaming down her freckled cheeks. Cradling her bulging belly with both arms, she clenched her teeth and whimpered like a wounded pup.

"I-I-I couldn't find anyone to . . . drive your truck," she managed with a grimace, "so . . ." she compressed her lips into a tight line.

"You drove it here yourself," Dugan finished for her. "You shouldn't have done that. Not when you're so close to having your baby."

The pitiful girl dug her fingernails into the chair's vinyl arms and squeezed through her teeth, "You . . . aren't . . . m-mad at . . . me, are you?"

"Hell, no." Dugan scooped his hat off his head and twisted the brim in his hands. "I'm just—that is—I mean I was afraid—"

"Dugan, do me a favor and get my bag out of the car, will you?" Claire asked in a calm voice. With Pamela Sue possibly in labor, the last thing either of them needed was an anxious, fretful Dugan.

With a quick nod, he sprinted for the door, as if thankful for an excuse to vacate the premises so he could calm his jangled nerves.

Pamela Sue's face was as red as a beet, her forehead damp with perspiration. Her carrot-red hair was plastered to her head like a damp cap. Claire smoothed a few damp strands from her forehead. "Well, well, did this baby decide it was tired of waiting?"

"I-I-I don't know," the teenager answered, the last word coming out of her wide open mouth as a scream.

"Pant now. Remember your classes. Pull up your legs," Claire coached, glancing at her watch. "That's it. When did the pains start?"

Panting like a veteran of childbirth, Pamela Sue endured the pain, then collapsed back into the chair.

"Good girl. Try to relax now." Claire peeled her watch from her wrist. "Here, take this. We need to time the period between contractions and the contractions themselves, just like we rehearsed."

"Yes, ma'am. But where's Lila? She's my partner. What am I going to do without my partner?"

"We'll call her in just a minute."

In her peripheral vision, Claire caught Dugan standing by the door, clutching her bag tightly. Tilting her head, she motioned him over while Pamela Sue talked.

"I delivered the vaccines to the barn, like Dugan said. On the way back, my . . ." she glanced up to find Dugan at her side. She lowered her eyelids shyly ". . . my water broke."

"Would you like Dugan to leave?" Claire asked, picking up on the embarrassed look on the girl's face.

"Oh, no. Please. I want him to stay. That is, if he's willing."

"You bet I am, Princess."

Claire shot him a glance of profound appreciation. She wondered if the impending arrival of Pamela Sue's baby there at the farm was conjuring up memories he, too, would just as soon forget.

"Matter of fact," Pamela Sue continued, "I was wondering if you'd do me a favor, Dugan."

"Anything you say."

"Do you suppose, well . . . would you mind, just for now . . . pretending you're the daddy?"

A flicker of panic flashed briefly in Dugan's eyes, but he quickly masked it. While Claire reeled from Pamela Sue's question, Dugan knelt

201

by the recliner and took the girl's hand. "If pretending I'm the daddy'll help, sure. I'd be proud to do it." He squeezed her hand.

"Thanks, Dugan. I won't tell anybody."

"You tell anybody you want. Now what do we have to do to have this baby?"

Claire's chest swelled with a new, deeper respect for this man who was capable of ignoring his own pain to help a frightened, lonely girl. She wanted to pull him aside and tell him so, but she had a baby to deliver.

"How long?" she repeated her question to Pamela Sue. "When did the pains start?"

"Twenty, thirty minutes ago. I'm not quite sure. I would have called, but I couldn't find the phone."

"In the bedroom," Dugan said, sheepishly hanging his head. "Living alone and all, I figured I didn't need more'n one."

In contrast, Claire had ordered four extensions for her new house.

"Dr. Linwood, it hurts so bad. Is it going to get any worse?" Pamela Sue gripped the arms of the chair and whimpered at the onset of another contraction.

Claire slid the watch from the grip of Pamela Sue's fingers. "Three minutes since the last one. Well, well, you're going to be a lucky little momma," Claire said, while inside she wanted to scream. She had no anesthesia, no forceps, no sterile conditions in which to deliver the baby. "Short labor the first time around."

Young and frightened by the prospect of giving birth, Pamela Sue had decided not to opt for natural childbirth, a decision Claire had endorsed. However, Claire had never dreamed they'd get stuck on Dugan's farm with the girl in hard labor, too far from the hospital in Lubbock to risk the drive.

With the contractions three minutes apart, Claire couldn't even risk the drive into the clinic where she could administer anesthesia. She was limited to the meager contents of her medical bag, unless she could somehow get the supplies at her clinic.

And then it hit her. Lila had all the keys. She was as familiar with the contents of the locked medications cabinet as she was.

"Dugan?"

"Yes?"

"I want you to make a call." She wrote "Get Lila" in big bold letters across a prescription pad, along with her aunt's phone number. Underneath that she scribbled a list of things she'd need from the clinic and thrust it into Dugan's hands. "Now."

"Sure thing, Doc."

"And if you don't mind, we'll deliver this baby right here in your recliner. It's as close to a birthing bed as they come. Just get me some clean sheets after you call Lila."

"Okey-doke."

"And now, I'm going to examine the momma-to-be." Noticing the girl had squeezed her eyes shut again, Claire crossed her fingers and silently mouthed, "Pray Lila makes it in time."

Pacing by his nightstand, Dugan listened to one ring, two, three, then perked up as he heard Lila's cheerful voice.

"Hello, this here's Lila."

"Lila, thank God you're—"

"I'm not home right about now. I'm on another mission of mercy."

Dugan dragged his hand down his face and listened to Lila's lengthy message, obviously left for Claire. She said Gunther had succumbed to another coughing fit about the time Dugan's foreman rolled into Sierra. Since the clinic was closed, the foreman had stopped at Lila's house for help.

Lila told Claire she wouldn't be attending the church social. She was driving into Lubbock with the foreman so she could watch over Gunther during the trip.

Dugan raked a hand through already disheveled hair. What in the hell would Claire do without the medications and instruments on her list? He couldn't leave her to drive into town. He'd left her before for help, when baby Angela had been working her way into the world. Before he'd returned, Claire had almost died, and Angela was too weak to fight the battle for her life.

204

Claire's nurses—of course! Maybe he could intercept one of them before the social began.

He tried both numbers, to no avail, and finally called the retired librarian who served as Claire's alternate receptionist. When no one answered, he broke out in a cold sweat. The church had never installed a phone in the hall where the dinner was taking place. He, Claire, and Pamela Sue were on their own.

Calm down, you fool, he lectured himself as he scooped up the freshly laundered linens Claire had requested. *It won't be like it was when Angela was born. Claire's a doctor. The girl's going to do just fine.*

Claire slipped on her rubber gloves, preparing to check Pamela Sue's dilation. From the thinness of the perineum around the vaginal opening, she knew this baby was ready to launch itself into this world.

Well, delivering a baby was like riding a bicycle, easy once a doctor learned. Nature did most of the work. She would just have to resort to vocal anesthesia and talk this sweet mother through the delivery.

Laying one palm over Pamela Sue's distended abdomen, she reached in to check her dilation. Her fingers collided with two tiny, slippery feet in the birth canal.

Breech. Oh, Lord. Pamela Sue's baby was breech. A double-foot lean, just like Angela had been.

She wanted to move, to go about delivering the baby, but her vision blurred. The sight, the smell, the texture of memories made her mind fuzzy.

A razor-sharp arrow of pain shot through her abdomen and worked its way around to her lower back. Her eyes focused again, but she wasn't in Dugan's sparsely furnished living room. She was—no! Not there. Not back in the wheat field alone. No doctor, no Dugan, only hawks circling overhead. Pain gripped Claire and tore the tender tissue between her legs where her precious baby was diving feet first into life.

Hot. Now cold. Shaking. Why couldn't she quit shaking? A cry? Her baby's. "Dugan! Where are you, Dugan?"

"Doc? Hey, Doc?"

Claire shook herself from her reverie and found Dugan gently squeezing her shoulder. He bent to whisper in her ear. "Better get a grip, Doc. You've got a baby to deliver."

"Baby." She swallowed hard and forced herself to take a deep breath. "Right. I'm fine. Just fine."

Dugan helped her position the clean linens around Pamela Sue. "You were thinking about Angela, weren't you?" he whispered.

She nodded, biting the tender flesh on the inside of her mouth to maintain her restored equilibrium.

"I guessed as much." Pulling her to her feet

for a moment, he looped an arm around her shoulder and hugged her comfortingly. "Don't think I'm not thinking about her, too. We couldn't do a blessed thing to help Angela. But this little tyke's going to make it. Pamela Sue has something you didn't. A doctor. Lila tells me I'm a fair-to-middlin' assistant. We're going to deliver the prettiest, the healthiest baby you've ever seen."

"Yes, that's what we're going to do," she confirmed, her resolve strengthening and her head clearing. "Did you get hold of Lila?"

"Nope. It's just you and me and the man upstairs, Doc."

"Let's hope we're enough," she prayed out loud.

Claire took a deep, bolstering breath, just in time. Pamela Sue's contractions were a minute apart. She was digging her fingernails into the arms of the chair and, bless her heart, trying not to scream.

Claire knelt before her on the oval braided rug, confidence flowing into her. Dugan positioned himself at the girl's side. She clung to Dugan's hand like a lifeline.

Knowing the urge to push would overwhelm Pamela Sue if she didn't concentrate and remember her lessons, Claire coached her in a soothing voice. "Blow, sweetheart. Puff out those pretty cheeks and pretend you're blowing out a fire. Yes, that's good. Hold off pushing until I give you the word. My, but you're a brave little mother."

Moving quickly, with skilled hands, Claire reached inside Pamela to free the umbilical cord from the baby's neck. "Ah, I feel the little dickens. You're about to have a beautiful baby."

Next came the episiotomy and the big moment. "Time to push, sweetheart. Try to relax your legs. Grab hold of Dugan's hand and push down and out, like you're scooting a basketball across the room."

Pamela Sue pushed. Claire deftly rotated the precious bundle of life feet first from the mother's womb into her practiced hands.

"A girl!" Dugan boomed. "We've got us a healthy baby girl."

Perfect arms and legs flexed. Eyes squinted against the light. Claire didn't have to stimulate this little one to take her first breath. The robust infant knotted her fists and let go of a lusty cry.

The baby might have been protesting the light, the cold, the harsh entry into her new world, but for Claire the cry was the sound of healing. The healthy wail of an infant who would grasp life and all it had to offer as Angela never could.

Smiling softly, she laid the child across Pamela Sue's abdomen and finished up the remaining delivery duties.

The tears were plentiful. On Pamela Sue's flushed cheeks, to be sure. On Dugan's, the proud surrogate daddy. And on Claire's. Certainly on Claire's. She'd delivered babies before, but she would never forget this child, her extraordinary birth and her healing powers.

Dugan lifted Claire's chin and kissed her softly, almost reverently on the lips. "Great job, Doc."

She smiled and kissed him back. "Thanks."

"We made a great team, didn't we?"

"We did at that."

"This calls for a celebration."

As if on cue, the baby flailed her tiny fists and let go of another lusty wail. Dugan chuckled. Claire cried. Pamela Sue stroked the buttocks of her minutes-old child.

This baby could wail all she wanted, Claire thought with a heart so full she was afraid it might burst right there in Dugan's living room.

Something somewhere summoned her to glance out the window, over the wide stretch of manicured grass to the carefully tended Nichols family plot. To the cherub perched atop Angela's grave marker. After all the years of painful reflection over what might have been, the grief released her.

"Thanks, Pamela Sue," she whispered and stroked her infant's head. "And thanks to you, tiny baby."

After she and Dugan had worked together to deliver Pamela Sue's baby, Claire longed to leap into his arms. She wanted to celebrate the joy they'd been denied years ago as parents.

But as soon as he carried mother and child into his spare bedroom, he insisted on driving into town for the supplies Pamela Sue needed. He took his dear, sweet time fetching diapers and baby bottles and the bag Pamela Sue had packed for the hospital. When he returned, he disappeared into the attic and emerged with Angela's old bassinet. He spent a whole hour scrubbing the white wicker.

He was so wrapped up in this baby, Claire was beginning to feel she could leave and he wouldn't notice.

With Pamela Sue and the baby resting peacefully in Dugan's spare bedroom, Claire washed up in the bathroom at the other end of the house. She was rebuttoning her blouse when she looked up and found Dugan leaning against the door frame. He regarded her with the softest of smiles.

"You look pooped," he observed.

"I could use a few winks," she admitted. *And the comfort of your arms.*

"Why don't you go crawl in my bed and take a nap. Better yet, spend the night. Hell, spend the weekend. You've got your beeper."

Claire would like nothing better than to accept his invitation, if it meant what she hoped it meant. "I don't know, Dugan."

"I hate to see you move Pamela Sue right now.

She's tired. She needs her rest. She could use your help."

"That's true, but . . ."

"If she'd given birth to that sweet baby in the hospital, she would have had a couple of doctors and a slew of nurses hovering over her for at least a day or two."

"That's true."

"And if you leave her here alone with me, the tongues in town will wag so hard they might fall out."

Claire chuckled. "Another truism."

"And if you stay, you could teach Pamela Sue how to diaper and burp and bathe the baby."

"The baby." Claire smiled at the mention of that sweet, carrot-haired infant lying on its back in the bassinet they'd bought for Angela.

"I'll admit staying here sounds a lot better than what I'd planned."

"Then the answer's yes?"

"Where would I sleep?" she asked boldly, for if she said yes to him, she needed to know all the question implied. Was he thinking strictly of the mother and baby? Or, Claire fervently hoped, did he have something more intimate in mind?

"In my bedroom, like I said."

Claire's heart flopped over in her chest. "And you?"

"On the couch."

"Oh, I see." She brushed past him into the

hallway, afraid her disappointment might show.

He caught her arm, drawing her close to him. "I promise not to bother you if you stay." His warm breath feathered across her cheek. The rough fabric of his jeans brushed against the hip of her skirt. Claire attempted to ignore the lightness that sprang to her limbs at the sudden, intimate contact, but she gave up trying.

She turned to lay her hands against the warmth of his chest. "That's not exactly the promise I wanted to—"

"Listen," he said, cocking an ear. "I think I hear a car."

"That's probably Lila."

"She'll be madder than a hornet she missed it all."

Lila made up for missing the birth by flouncing around the house, tidying this, readying that for the baby. Claire stood back and watched Dugan help, feeling more and more estranged from him. By his euphoric mood and the pride that swelled his chest whenever he picked up the baby, she would have sworn the child was truly his.

After a late dinner Lila patted a loud burp from the baby and tucked her into her bassinet. Claire walked Lila to the door. "Why don't you come back with me and spend the night?" Lila said.

"I think I'll stick around here a while. Make sure Pamela Sue and the baby do okay."

Lila eyed her suspiciously, then shook her head. "Can't say I blame you. I'll be out in the mornin' with formula and a fresh gown for the little momma. You call if you need anything else, you hear?"

Claire stood at the kitchen window the next morning, staring numbly into the backyard at sunrise. She hadn't slept more than an hour or two, between checking on Pamela Sue and the baby and listening for Dugan. He kept his promise, however, and never crawled into bed with her.

Coffee cup in hand, she looked at the old frame house out back where they had lived. Why hadn't he torn it down, used the lumber for firewood?

And there, beside the ramshackle house, was Old Ruby.

Ruby. What pleasures she and Dugan had shared in that rusting heap of a truck. She couldn't help but smile while her gaze roamed over its contours. After their senior prom, they'd ridden in Ruby to Joseph Witcomb's north forty and made love for the first time.

If Dugan was so frugal, why hadn't he sold Ruby for scrap metal, if nothing else?

"Mornin', early bird."

Claire whirled around, sloshing coffee onto her hand as she turned. "Ouch! Oh, Dugan, I didn't know you were up."

213

"Better put ice on that." He grabbed a few ice cubes from the freezer, wrapped them in a washcloth, and handed them to her. He paused as their fingers touched for a fleeting second. His gaze lifted to the open neck of the blue Western shirt he'd loaned her to sleep in. The shirt covered her buttocks, but just barely.

Dugan wore only a pair of jeans, with the top button unfastened. Claire's gaze flicked to his bare chest and the black swirls of hair she would love to rake her fingers through.

If Dugan intended to keep his distance from her, he'd chosen a poor way to start the day.

"I . . . uh . . . noticed you still have Old Ruby."

His gaze swept to the window. In the soft rays of early sunlight a smile stole over his face, then quickly faded. "I couldn't bring myself to sell the old girl."

"Why not?"

"I . . . uh . . . decided to keep her because the rabbits keep hatching their young underneath her."

The realization that even Dugan's truck was more fertile than she was stung.

And then it struck her. Maybe that's why Dugan was really reluctant to welcome her back into his life. Because she couldn't give him the children he wanted.

Even though he told Claire he loved her, even though he might feel that honest emotion, maybe in the process of helping her deliver Pamela Sue's baby, he'd figured out loving wasn't enough.

"I'll have breakfast ready in twenty minutes," she announced sharply and turned to open the refrigerator.

"The baby's up." He gazed out the window again, a yearning in his expression. "I took her to her momma."

Claire busied herself assembling the makings of breakfast. She refused to look at Dugan, for tears were clouding her eyes. "What are your plans for the day?"

Dugan poured himself a tall glass of milk and leaned back against the counter nearby—too near for Claire to think logically. "My foreman volunteered to cover me for the day. So, I thought I'd hang around, in case you gals needed me."

"Well, I plan to leave after breakfast," she announced.

His hand shot out, capturing her upper arm. "Don't, Claire."

"Don't what?"

"Leave."

She thrust her chin in the air and stared at him icily. "Why shouldn't I?"

"Because I want you to stay."

She shrugged out of his grasp. "You don't need me."

"Who says?" he demanded.

215

"I do, damnit."

"Are you afraid what the town gossips will say about us if you stay?"

How could one man be so insensitive and dumb. "They'll talk about me whether I'm here or not. Why do you want me to stay anyway? Lila'll be back in a couple of hours."

"Why? I'll tell you why." He slammed his glass on the counter and pulled her into his arms.

She met his lips in a kiss of desperation. Tongues and hopes and heartache tangled in their wet open mouths.

Dugan tasted of milk and everything that had ever made sense to Claire. She was trembling when he broke the kiss and tacked on, "Because if you leave, I won't have the chance to hold you like this . . . and pretend."

Claire slumped against his chest. "Pretend what?"

He tucked her head beneath his chin and rumpled the tangled mass of hair with his hand. "Pretend I never sent you away."

She moved her fists between their chests and pushed against him, but he wouldn't release her. "Dugan, I can't do this."

"What? Be near me?"

"If you only knew how much I wanted to be near you."

The dimple plunged deep into his cheek. His hands slid down over the curve of her hips, pulling her flush against him. Against the clear evidence the town gossips weren't what was occupying his mind. "Then lighten up, Doc. The weekend's too short for fretting."

Dugan had never been happier in his life, except for those first few months with Claire, before the hard times and fatigue etched fine lines in her young face.

Together they changed diapers and bathed the baby Pamela Sue couldn't decide what to name. Every time Dugan heard the infant's lusty cry, he bolted for the spare bedroom and plucked her from Angela's bassinet. Every time he handed the kid to Claire, she glowed as she held her.

Because of him, Claire had been denied the pleasure of bearing any more children. However, this one weekend she could enjoy the newborn experience through Pamela Sue's little one.

He poked his head into the girl's room and found her watching MTV on the television set he'd moved from the living room. "Have you seen Claire?"

"She took the baby a few minutes ago," Pamela Sue told him. "For a bath, I think."

A bath. He loved baby bath time. He adored watching the little doll gaze up at Claire with wide, unfocused eyes while she cleansed every crease and crevice in the perfect pink body. Were all babies that pretty, or was he smitten by Red?

Red. That's what he'd call her, after the hair

217

she'd been blessed with by her mother.

Claire wasn't in the bathroom, nor in the kitchen. He found the door to his bedroom ajar. He peeked in, and his spirits soared straight through the ceiling.

Claire was curled up in his bed on her side, sound asleep. Red lay nestled in the curve of her arm, her little cupid mouth working in that cute sucking motion while she slept.

He tiptoed in and stood at the foot of the bed. His heart filled with more pride than a man who wasn't the baby's father had a right to feel.

He knew Red would go home tomorrow, but he was determined to be part of her life. He'd help Pamela Sue with clothes and school expenses and establish a college fund at Orville's bank. Someday Pamela Sue would probably marry, and he'd bow to the couple's wishes — get lost, if that's what they wanted. Most of the time anyway.

He just longed to give Red what Angela had never had.

Claire fluttered her lashes dreamily and smiled. "Hmm. Dugan. What are you doing?"

"Watching my two favorite girls."

"You want your bed?"

If you're in it, he wanted to tell her. *And not one night, but forever.*

She knew how he felt, though. He'd told her in plain English he couldn't bear to make love to her and walk away. He'd been waiting for a signal that she shared his feelings, but so far nothing.

"Stay where you are," he told her and rounded the foot of the bed.

"She was fretting. That's why I brought her in here and—"

"You don't have to explain, Claire. I understand."

He sank down beside her on the mattress, then scooched up behind her and warmed her back with his chest. She didn't complain when he slung one leg over hers, even though he still wore his cowboy boots.

The black ones. Did she remember he'd worn them when they were married?

"You've kept those boots all these years."

He glanced down at the black leather and slid his arm around her waist. "I couldn't get rid of them. I wore them when I married the most wonderful woman on the face of the earth. You taught me to love, Claire. You taught me I could trust a woman. I don't know what I would've done if you'd never come into my life."

"Do you ever hear from your mother, or your dad?" Claire asked him.

"Nope. I gave up hopin' a long time ago. I finally accepted the fact some folks aren't meant to be parents. But enough talk about them. I just want to lie here and be close to you."

He wiggled his hand between her and Red, and closed his palm over Claire's breast. Heaven in his hand. She murmured a soft sigh.

If he and Claire could ever find a meeting ground, they could marry, adopt a baby someday. Then this could be their family lying on this bed.

He lifted one of Red's tiny hands and curled her digits over his forefinger. He'd never forget this little one, even if he was lucky enough to be a daddy himself someday.

Claire glanced over her shoulder and smiled. God, how he loved that smile.

"You like her, don't you?"

"Yeah, I'd say she's a keeper."

"You would have made a wonderful father, Dugan. I'm surprised you haven't married and filled this house with children."

He rubbed his chin over the softness of her cheek. "No one could measure up to you."

"Well, maybe someday you'll get to be a daddy."

"You've missed something, sweetheart." He kissed the tip of her perky nose. "First comes the loving. Then comes the baby."

Chapter Ten

Pamela Sue's baby snuggled close to Claire's chest. In frantic searching movements, she instinctively groped for a nipple to suckle.

Through the soft cotton of Claire's pink turtleneck and her lace bra, she felt the gentle tugging of the sweet, innocent mouth. If only she could provide the baby with the nourishment she sought.

"I'm afraid you're wasting your energy, little one," Claire murmured and stroked her soft, rounded cheek with the back of her finger.

"Red," Dugan said. "I'm calling her Red until Pamela Sue comes up with a name."

"Red," Claire repeated, thinking of the baby's flaming hair so much like her mother's. "Red suits her."

With her forefinger Claire reluctantly broke the vacuum of Red's mouth. The infant's face screwed into a red-faced frown, and she wailed with healthy lungs.

"I'll take her," Dugan offered, which didn't surprise Claire. He couldn't seem to get enough of Red. He had already learned to diaper her, feed her water from a bottle, and burp the little tyke by inching up her spine with gently massaging fingers.

He scooped the baby into a confident one-hand hold and tucked her at his side as if she were a small bag of feed. He tackled his share of the baby-sitting chores as he tackled everything else in his life—with a fierce determination to succeed and to enjoy the pursuit.

She watched his eyes sparkle as he lifted Red before his face to make soft clucking sounds. Claire wished Dugan's grandfather could see him now. He was a man strong enough to build the struggling dirt farm into a thriving, debt-free ranching operation, yet gentle enough to calm a fretting baby. A rare combination.

Claire's heart swelled with pride for the man Dugan had grown to be, or maybe the man he'd been all along, if she'd given him the chance to show her. She loved him more than she'd ever thought possible. And to think the miracle of birth she'd shared with him had broken down the wall of her tightly constructed defenses.

Lying there in Dugan's bed, she realized she had so much to tell him before Sunday evening

222

arrived and they both returned to their separate lives.

"Dugan?"

"Yeah, Doc?"

"I owe you a big thanks."

"For what?" he asked, turning away from Red with a questioning stare.

"For helping me and Pamela Sue. And Red there."

"Heck, Doc. Can't you see I'm having the time of my life?" He looked at her strangely. Then he whirled around and strode to the door, tossing over his shoulder, "Might be a good time to grab a few winks," before he disappeared down the hall.

What the heck? "Dugan?"

Already out the door and down the hall, Dugan halted and backed up several steps. Damn. He'd almost made it. He'd whipped out of the room fast so Claire couldn't tell how just lying in bed with her, just seeing her sprawled across the chenille spread, affected him and his snug jeans.

He backed up a few steps and stuck his head around the doorway — only his head. "You want something, Doc?"

"I'm not sleepy. I don't want a nap."

"Well then why don't you come along and keep Pamela Sue company while this one has her lunch?"

"I don't want to do that either."

Shifting the fretting baby to his shoulder, Dugan frowned. "What do you want to do, Doc? Read? Watch television?"

Even a fool could tell Claire had more on her inventive mind than talking, reading, or watching television. Wanting to chew the fat didn't make a woman's eyelids ride low and sultry like hers were now. The thought of intelligent conversation didn't make her blue eyes smolder either.

If he were another man, he'd probably sample what she was offering and do them both a favor. Instead, he'd probably hook his toes under the living room sofa and do two or three hundred sit-ups.

"What I want to do is, uh . . . talk to you about something," Claire was saying. She spoke with that telling husky quality to her voice he recalled from way back when.

"Yeah, well, okay." He kissed the back of Red's fuzzy head. "I'm a bit busy. It can wait, can't it?"

"Not too long."

Dugan gulped and steadied the baby in his shaking hands. "Okay, Doc. Be back soon as I get Red settled in with her momma."

Claire watched fifty-six minutes creep by on the bedside clock. Fifty-six. She noted every one of them and wondered what was taking so long to deliver Red to Pamela Sue's tender breasts.

The longer Claire waited, the more her stomach flip-flopped like the perch she and Dugan used to catch in his pond. She'd begun to think he wasn't coming back for their . . . talk.

If he didn't, she'd track him down like the hordes of quail hunters that flocked to Sierra. She'd force him to listen to what she had to say.

For the past twenty-four hours she'd fought a valiant battle with the dictates of her heart—and finally admitted defeat. She knew she loved Dugan with a fierceness that defied description. He'd crept into her soul and pried her heart from its lonely moorings.

"So," he said, reappearing in the doorway but not stepping one foot into the room. "What do you want to . . . talk about?"

Claire rolled to her side. Elbow buried deep in the feather pillow that bore Dugan's drugging scent, she propped her head in her open palm. "Did Red nurse?"

"Tried to."

"Pamela Sue's milk should come in soon."

"I gave her a bottle for back-up."

"Where are they now?"

"Both sleeping."

"Come in then and close the door," Claire told him.

"Doc," he said, curling his fingers tightly around the doorframe, "don't start something. Not if you don't plan to finish what you start."

"Dugan?"

"Yes?"

"Are you going to stand there all day?"

"Well, now, that depends."

"On what?"

"On what you've got to say."

She patted the spot beside her on the bedspread. "Come on over and sit down. I'd like you a bit closer than ten feet away when I tell you this."

His eyes lit up like the stars they used to watch, lying flat on their backs in the meadow. "Tell me what?"

"Do I have to pry your hands off that door frame?"

Dugan hung his head. The clock on the nightstand ticked away the seconds.

When he lifted his head, determination had hardened his features. He crossed his arms over his chest. His chin shot up. "Just go ahead and tell me what you have to say."

"You know, don't you?"

"I have to hear you say it. I won't budge until you do."

Claire flicked a speck of lint from the bedspread and screwed up her courage. Now that her chance had finally arrived, she could hardly speak. Her heart pounded as if she were about to deliver a speech before the medical society. But no speech in her life could be as important as the simple words she was about to say.

"I love you, Dugan."

A muscle in his jaw twitched. "Say it again.

I want to make sure I heard you right."

"I said, 'I love you.' "

Dugan ducked inside the room and shut the door behind him with the heel of his boot. A silly grin crept across his face. His dimple plunged to record depths. His chest swelled, and he ran his tongue over his lips, lips Claire needed to feel claim hers.

He took one step, but halted, his smile fading in a furrowed frown. "The past's forgiven?"

Claire walked her fingers across the bed and reached out to him with her heart, a smile, and an open palm. "What past?"

He chuckled. "Something about fourteen years and a peck of trouble."

"Forgiven. Nothing could be as bad as living the rest of my life without ever loving you again."

In three more steps Dugan was standing beside the bed. He hitched a hip onto the mattress. It shifted under his weight. He sat there for a moment, another eternity, searching Claire's eyes before he reached over and pressed his fingers gently to the valley between her breasts. "Loving as in here, in your heart?"

"In my heart. In my mind." She reached up and snagged his neck in the crook of her arm. "In my body. Dugan, if you don't make love to me, I think I'm going to die."

Dugan flattened his palms on either side of her head. Hovering inches from her face, he gazed deep into her eyes. "I didn't think I'd ever hear you say that again. I'm so excited, I—Hell, come here, woman."

Like Claire, he poured into his kiss the pent-up frustration of too many sleepless nights. She'd dreamed of such an embrace, but until that moment she hadn't realized why her life had been so empty. All those years she'd been aching to touch Dugan again, to vent her soul in selfless giving.

Outside a cow brayed in the pasture. The afternoon sun slid closer to the western horizon. On the other side of the house, Red lay in the bassinet, sucking her fist while her mother slumbered nearby.

Claire focused her attention solely on Dugan. She didn't reflect for a moment on her wants and needs. Instead she trained her heart on the dear man who covered her trembling body with his and pressed her deep into the downy softness of the mattress.

Twelve years of loneliness and frustration exploded in their first desperate kiss. Claire whimpered into Dugan's mouth but gave him no evidence of pain, only hands and lips and tongue urging him closer, deeper.

Mere seconds had ticked away since she'd confessed what he'd known in his heart for weeks. But she was already trembling—her hands frantically tearing at the back of his shirt. The trembling spread to her arms, to her thighs, and, he sensed, that womanly part of her he wanted to bury himself in.

"Oh, Dugan, I've missed you so much."

"I know. I've thought about holding you like this every damned night for twelve years."

"Is the door locked?"

"Sure as heck is."

"Good." She squirmed beneath his weight and slipped her hands beneath his shirt to rake the hard muscles straining across his back.

He rolled over, pulling Claire with him to sit astride his lower abdomen. Through the thickness of her weathered jeans, that secret part of her pressed against his stomach. Was she wearing the pink bikini panties that had disappeared from the shower rod that morning? He couldn't wait to see, to strip them from her lovely body.

Not yet, old boy. Go slow. Make the glory last.

That fuzzy self-admonition floated around in Dugan's brain like a lost child. He had every intention of taking his time sliding her turtleneck up her torso, kissing each stretch of freshly exposed skin. It would be like unwrapping a long-desired present.

But Claire, ah, sweet, bold Claire, popped the bottom two snaps on his shirt and bent to flick her tongue over the skin above his navel. He reached behind her head and released the catch on her pearl barrette. He threaded his hands into her silky hair and wadded the golden locks

229

in his fists. Claire was his again, her heart, her body. He prayed he was strong enough for the strain of total pleasure.

"I always loved the way you tasted," she murmured, her breath hot against his skin.

Restraint snapped; resolve dissolved in a rush of need to touch Claire's skin. He tugged the hem of her knit blouse from inside her jeans and peeled off the top.

Claire's full breasts strained against the pink lace of her skimpy bra. Only a delicate front closure held the garment against her body.

Hands trembling, he released the hook and her breasts fell free of their constraint.

Claire hooked her thumbs beneath the straps and, arching her back, slid it up over her head. With a snap of her hand, the lingerie sailed somewhere to the floor. Dugan didn't care where. He only knew he lifted heaven in his hands, Claire's silky breasts.

While Dugan pleasured himself, she dispensed with his shirt and let it slide from her fingers over the side of the bed. She threw her head back and moaned at the exquisite aching his circling thumbs brought to her distended nipples. As she straddled Dugan's abdomen, insistent contractions seized her there between her thighs.

"Ah, Claire, why did we wait so long?"

She opened her eyes and smoothed her hands over the contours of Dugan's magnificent chest. Like Claire's, his nipples were hard and begging to be touched. He moaned as she lightly smoothed her fingers over them.

"We waited so it could be like this. As good as before." She bent to flick his nipple with her tongue. "No, better."

Dugan growled like a wild animal. That's how he felt. But a wild animal didn't wear cowboy boots or half the clothes that kept him from blending his body with Claire's.

Hands on her waist, Dugan lifted Claire and gentled her down beside him on the bed. First Claire's clothes, then his. That's what he wanted. Then he could soak up the beauty of her naked flesh and glowing face while he stripped the rest of his confounded clothes from his aching body.

One by one the garments fell away, his boots, Claire's jeans, his. They knelt in the ribbons of afternoon sun slanting across the bed and laced their arms around each other's neck.

A speck of shyness glistened in Claire's eyes. Dugan remembered what pleased her, what drove her to the brink of ecstasy, and he gladly led her there. When at last he permitted himself to enter her, she was hot and wet and ready and begging to feel him inside.

Their coupling was desperate, yet gentle and giving. Claire cried out at the precise moment Dugan shattered inside her. They lay in each other's arms, passion spent, hearts bursting from the exquisite mutual giving of a man and woman. Their love had not only survived but flourished a second, blessed time.

"Worth the wait," Dugan mumbled and drew Claire closer to his chest.

"Hmm. I agree."

"Say it again."

"I agree."

"No, the other."

She lifted her chin and grinned. "I love you, Dugan. I always have. I always will."

"Then what do you say we make up for a little more lost time?" he murmured and slid his hand between her parted thighs.

If time had flown in Cancún for Claire and Dugan, the hours rode the speed of sound that weekend.

Every time Pamela Sue and Red drifted off to sleep at the same time, Claire and Dugan bolted to the privacy of his bedroom. In the afterglow of their lovemaking, they cooked, laundered, and even folded the tiny baby garments Lila had delivered to the farm.

Dugan told Claire how he'd expanded his herd, then sold when the price of beef was high. How he'd raised horses and grown cotton, sweet potatoes, peanuts, and wheat, and crop-dusted in the next county. If there was a dollar to be made, he didn't sit around thinking about

232

it.

Claire shared the struggles of medical school with Dugan, and stories of the pranks she and her sister students had pulled on the professors. She told him how she had pretended to be a cadaver and almost scared one professor into cardiac arrest. How she'd memorized until she thought every cell in her brain was crammed with the names of body parts and medical terminology.

So much to catch up on in the course of the twenty-four hours left in the weekend.

"I've got a confession," Dugan admitted Saturday night over coffee in the living room.

"You're keeping another woman in the barn."

"Get serious."

She shrugged. "Lila did you say you were seeing someone in Amarillo."

"Oh, her. She was more a friend than anything else."

"Was?" Claire asked pointedly.

"I haven't seen her or called her since you returned for the interview. I take that back. I called to tell her about you."

"Good. For me, that is. I'm sure she was ticked off."

"Actually, she understood. She said whenever I drove over to see her, I never came alone. I always had you with me, in my heart, that is."

Dugan set his coffee mug on the end table

and took Claire's hand in his. "I don't want to talk about her. I've got a couple things I need to get off my mind."

"Like?"

"Like I'm sorry for treating you like you had sawdust for brains."

Claire laughed. "Which time?"

"Lots of times. But specifically, I'm referring to the way I talked down to you about how you handle your money."

"Oh, that. You should apologize."

"I didn't mean to be . . ."

"Condescending?"

"Yeah. That's it. Condescending."

"I can see how you'd be concerned, after your grandfather dug himself so deeply in debt. But I'm not your grandfather, Dugan. I've supported myself all these years. Not in a fancy manner, mind you, but I did get by."

"I know. I should have kept my big mouth shut."

"Apology accepted."

"How do you think Pamela Sue's going to manage with Red to support? She's not even out of high school."

"It won't be easy," Claire admitted.

"I've tried to get her to talk about it. Every time I do, she changes the subject. How does Lila feel about her staying?"

"She doesn't mind, but then you know Lila. She'd adopt a busload of orphans if her budget allowed."

"I plan to help Pamela Sue. That's something else I wanted to tell you."

"How do you plan to do that?"

"A little money now and then. A trust fund for Red."

"Pamela Sue may resent hand-outs."

"Not if Red's hungry."

"We'll see," Claire murmured and snuggled her back against Dugan's broad chest. "Before she leaves tomorrow, we'll both go in and talk about lots of things."

Actually, Pamela Sue did the talking. At noon on Sunday, she called Claire and Dugan into the living room. Still in a dither over her failed attempts at nursing, she sat there, rocking briskly in the recliner.

"Hi, kid," Dugan said, ruffling her red hair.

Claire noticed she'd made an attempt to style it. She'd drawn the wavy length into a bright yellow bow at the side of her head. She'd dressed in a loose, flowing dress Lila had bought her. So young to be a mother, Claire thought. She sat beside Dugan on the couch, prepared to bolster the girl's flagging courage.

"I've been thinking," Pamela Sue began and bit her lip hard before continuing. "About a lot of things."

"What things?" Claire encouraged her.

"Red mostly."

"You're going to call her Red?"

"I'm not going to call her anything."

Claire exchanged worried glances with Dugan and waited for her to elaborate.

"I don't want you to think I don't love her." Tears sprang to the young mother's eyes. "I love her something fierce-like."

Dugan leaned forward and braced his elbows on his knees. "What are you trying to tell us, Princess?"

"What I'm trying to say is, I've decided to give her up for adoption."

Dugan sprang from the couch, his brown eyes wide, disbelieving. "You . . . you can't do that."

Pamela Sue's chin quivered. "I can, and I will."

"But, Pamela Sue, if it's money, I've already told Claire I'm willing to help. Tell her Claire. Tell her what we talked about last night."

"That's right," Claire said. "Dugan wants to help."

"And no strings attached."

Pamela Sue pushed out of the recliner gingerly and moved to the picture window that overlooked the grassy span sloping to the road. "I can't give her what she needs."

"You can give her love. That's the most important thing," Claire said, understanding the overwhelming burden of responsibility facing Pamela Sue.

"But what about clothes and books and what about a home?"

"Lila said you could live with her as long as you like."

"Eighteen years? Red's going to need a home for at least that long." Her voice broke. "I don't want her to end up like me. No place to call home. Nothing in her pocket but dreams."

"Why don't you wait a couple of weeks before you make your decision," Claire advised. "Post-partum blues are normal. Your hormones are way out of kilter."

"Two weeks won't change my mind." The girl's chin shot up. Claire had to admire the brave sacrifice Pamela Sue was willing to make for the sake of her precious child.

From the spare bedroom, a soft whimper grew into Red's impatient wail. Claire rose from the couch to comfort her and to ease the ache the mere thought of seeing Red disappear brought to her own heart.

"Wait," Pamela Sue said. "I want to get her this time."

Neither Dugan nor Claire said anything until she'd left the room. But as soon as she was out of earshot, Dugan paced the braided rug before the fireplace.

"What do you make of all this?" he asked, raking a hand through shiny black hair Claire had trimmed an hour ago.

"She is young, Dugan. She has her whole life in front of her. If this is her decision, we have to honor it."

"I can't bear to think of Red living somewhere else, somewhere we can't see her." He cast a forlorn glance in the direction of his spare bedroom. "As it is, I'm going to be downright miserable after Pamela Sue goes home with Lila tonight and you go back to the hotel."

At the sound of Pamela Sue's bare feet padding on the hall's hardwood floors, Dugan and Claire ended their discussion.

When Pamela Sue entered the room, she had Red propped over her shoulder. The little angel was wearing a yellow stretch suit Lila had bought as a coming-home outfit. Pamela Sue patted her back. Red burped loudly and rooted at her mother's breast.

Pamela Sue lowered Red to cradle her in her arms. Claire's heart ached for the child-woman caught between two worlds.

"As I said, I've done a lot of thinking," Pamela Sue continued, with that proud jut to her chin. "I'm sixteen. I need an education. That way, when I have another baby someday, I can support her." Her lower lip trembled. Claire resisted the urge to go to her.

"I've learned a lot, thanks to you, Dr. Linwood. Because you hired me and taught me stuff that'll help me get a job. I'd like to go home . . . to Albuquerque. Finish school. Get a job. Maybe even go to college."

"But how will you live?" Dugan demanded. "How will you eat?"

"There's places. It won't be no picnic, but I figure if you can do what you did here on the farm, I can rough it, too."

"How did she know . . . ?" Dugan started to ask, but Pamela Sue shushed him.

"Someday I want to help people like you do, Dr. Linwood. I don't know if I have the brains to be no doctor. But I figure I could be a nurse maybe."

"You can be anything you set your mind to," Claire said.

"I want the best for Red."

"I'll start the adoption proceedings as soon as you say," Claire said regretfully, "but please, do as I ask and wait those two weeks. If you haven't changed your mind by then, I'm sure there'll be hundreds of couples, right here in Texas, who would make loving parents for Red."

"I don't want just any parents."

"I understand. I'll hire an attorney to make sure she winds up in a good, loving home."

"No, you don't understand."

Dugan frowned and crossed to sit beside Claire. He took her hand and squeezed it. She appreciated his sensitivity. She didn't want to see Red disappear from their lives anymore than he did. They weren't actual relatives of Pamela Sue's or Red's, but she felt the

239

connection nonetheless.

"What don't we understand?" Dugan asked.

"I said, 'I don't want just any parents.' " She smiled down at her baby, kissed the tip of Red's button nose, then relinquished her to Claire.

"What I want," Pamela Sue said, with a lingering hold on Red's balled up fist, "is for you and Dugan to be her momma and daddy."

Chapter Eleven

"You want what?" Dugan blurted out.

"I want you and Dr. Linwood to be Red's momma and daddy. You can call her Red if you like, or you can pick another name."

"Being parents involves a lot more than picking a name," Claire managed to mumble, but her head was spinning from Pamela Sue's request.

She wanted Claire to be this precious baby's mother. She wanted Dugan to be the father. The inherent assumptions were overwhelming.

"You could do it. You could be good parents. I've watched you this weekend. I think you love Red as much as I do."

"Even so . . ." Claire started to counter.

"And Red would be the luckiest kid in the world. Two big houses to pick from."

"You're overlooking something," Claire said,

241

but even as she brought up the point, she cradled the innocent infant closer to her breast.

"What's that?"

"Dugan and I aren't married."

"So."

"So, it would be difficult for us to be her parents."

"I may not have a high school diploma yet, Dr. Linwood, but I'm not dumb."

"No one said you were dumb, Princess," Dugan consoled her. "You're anything but dumb."

"And I can see more'n you think."

"Meaning what?" Claire inquired.

"I can see you love Dugan, and he loves you." Her chin quivered. "I hope someday I'm lucky enough to be in love like you, with a man who'll love me back."

Claire focused her attention on Red, pretending to fuss with the baby's flyaway hair so she would not have to look at Dugan. She knew, especially after this weekend, how much he wanted a child in his life. Hadn't she told him herself what a wonderful father he'd make? And he'd said to her in many ways over the past several weeks he wanted to resume their marriage.

Still, he hadn't asked her to marry him. Even after she'd told him she loved him and after they'd made love not once but several times. If anything, he'd chosen the strangest times to distance himself from her. If he proposed now, could she believe he wanted her as his wife? Or did he only want the opportunity to be a father that their marriage would assure him?

"Claire—Doc—and I have a lot of things to work through before we could consider marrying," Dugan said, confirming Claire's suspicions. "We can't guarantee you we'd wind up together."

Dugan's words blistered her ears. She wanted him to tell Pamela Sue he'd think about her request. That he'd talk the idea over with Claire and get back to her. Or she would have been satisfied if he'd moved to sit beside her on the couch and said he wanted to marry her more than anything in the world. That if she would consider his proposal, they would consider the teenager's request.

But he just stood there, hands on hips, staring out the window as if trying to decide whether he wanted Claire to be his wife after all.

Well, she would save him the embarrassment and herself the heartache of another rejection. She searched frantically for a reason why Pamela Sue's request wouldn't work and found one.

"There's something else to think about," she said.

"What?" Pamela Sue asked.

"I hired you. I made sure you had a job during your pregnancy. Then I delivered Red. There are some who would accuse me of manipulating you so I could . . ." she paused, the thought of

243

what she was about to say disgustingly repugnant, ". . . so I could buy your baby."

"Lila has a perfect word for that thinking. Hogwash!" the young mother said.

"I'm not sure any judge would agree," Claire said, yet she desperately wanted to raise this child cradled in her arms. And she wanted to raise her with the man she loved.

Dugan.

She glanced up to find he'd resumed pacing, his eyes dark and brooding. At the lull in the conversation, he stopped abruptly as if a light bulb had clicked on in his brain. He crossed his arms tightly over his chest, over the blue Western shirt with three buttons unsnapped, and studied Claire with a narrowed gaze.

What had she done to deserve such a cold, probing expression?

As if she wanted to contribute her two cents' worth, Red flailed her arms and commenced screaming.

"There, there, baby, don't fret," Claire cooed and lifted her to her shoulder. "We want to be rocked, do we?" she asked and lifted the squirming bundle to her shoulder. "I'm going to put her down now. We can finish this later."

"I'm hungry," Pamela Sue announced, as if she hadn't just made the single most important announcement of her life. "Mind if I poke around in the fridge?"

Food, Dugan thought. How could the girl

think about food at a moment like this? Yet her hunger gave him an excuse to seek the privacy he needed.

"Sit. I'll get you something," he told her and wandered into the kitchen in a daze.

When Pamela Sue had dropped her bomb about wanting to give Red up for adoption, he'd felt like punching his fist through the wall. That little angel was part of him now. Pamela Sue couldn't give her away.

This morning he'd snuck out to the barn for an hour while the three girls were sleeping. He'd found an old burlap sack and fashioned it into a carrier. This would allow him to strap the little tyke to his chest and ride the pasture with her. Fresh air was supposed to be good for babies.

He figured in a couple of weeks Pamela Sue would be ready for a break. He'd offer to baby-sit for the day. He wanted to be ready when the opportunity presented itself.

When Pamela Sue made that first announcement, panic had knotted up his gut. He knew he wasn't Red's father. He hadn't even thought about trying to substitute for the real thing, but he couldn't bear to think of strangers taking her away to God knows what kind of place.

Then when Pamela Sue had told them she wanted him and Claire to be Red's momma and daddy, she'd almost knocked him off his feet. For a fleeting moment, he'd thought she was some angel who'd descended from heaven with the one gift he and Claire couldn't give each other—a child.

He'd turned to Claire, his heart bursting with joy. He'd expected to see tears streaming down her cheeks. He'd expected her to hug the heck out of him and tell Pamela Sue, for both of them, she wouldn't be sorry for her decision.

Instead, she'd avoided him like he'd rolled in cow manure. Then, to boot, she'd thrown up some stupid smoke screen about doctor ethics.

Hell, if she wanted Red bad enough, they'd find a way to beat the courts and medical ethics. He'd sell his herd and hire the best lawyer in the state if he had to.

What was the real reason for Claire's hesitation? Didn't she love him enough to marry him? Hadn't their weekend together meant anything to her but good sex?

He didn't get the answers to his questions. Not from Claire anyway. She made herself scarce the rest of the afternoon, until Lila flitted into the house at five. Lila bore a big grin, a new car seat for Red, and a big pot of stew for dinner.

"Where is that precious thing?" she asked Dugan. "I can't wait to get her home." She glanced around the empty living room. "Where's everybody?"

"Oh, here and there," he said glumly.

Lila gave him one of her famous hugs.

"There, there. It isn't the end of the world. She'll be back, mark my word."

"She who?" Dugan asked.

"Why Claire, of course."

"Oh, Claire."

Lila regarded him with wise eyes. "You two have a tiff or somethin'?"

Dugan didn't want to be the one to tell her about Pamela Sue's plans. He didn't feel like talking at all. He made a feeble excuse for his foul mood and excused himself to check the feeding troughs in the barn.

Dinner was a disaster. Not the stew. The stew was delicious as usual. But Dugan had never sat through a meal quieter than a funeral wake. He sat at the head of the table, poking at the potatoes and the plump cubes of beef. At the foot of the table, Claire stared at her plate, her habitual smile replaced by a grim expression. He tried to make conversation. "Hey, Doc, how's the house comin' along?"

"Fine," she said and made a telltale swipe at her eyes with her napkin. Was she crying?

"I suppose you'll be buyin' furniture soon."

She expelled a deep breath and glanced up. She looked miserable. "I've hired a decorator to do that for me."

"Who?" he asked, trying like hell to keep the conversation going.

"Someone in Dallas the builder told me about."

"You could of used the locals. Rebecca Torrington or Jamie Hurst," he commented.

"I was afraid since there were two decorators in town, I'd cause trouble if I picked one over the other."

Dugan shook his head. "You could have split it up, Doc."

Claire shot him a go-to-hell look and stared back at her plate.

Lila clanked her spoon in her bowl. "Will somebody please tell me what's goin' on around here? It feels like a darned deep freeze."

Silence.

"The stew bad?"

"No, it's delicious," Claire said. As if to prove her opinion, she spooned a bite of stew into her mouth.

"Do I have to squeeze it out of you?" Lila insisted.

Pamela Sue lifted her chin and looked first to Dugan, then to Claire. "They're mad at me."

"Why?"

"We're not mad at you," Dugan assured her.

"Then why all this hostility?" Lila asked.

"Because I want to give Red up for adoption," Pamela Sue announced bravely.

"You want to what?" Lila shrieked.

"I want Red to have a good home, with a mother and a father."

"Red? Who's Red?"

"Dugan nicknamed the baby Red," Claire explained.

"Hell of a name for a little one. Be that as it may, why the sudden decision to give your baby up, child?" she asked the teenager. "You can live with me as long as you like."

"Eighteen years?" she queried, and Dugan listened to the earlier conversation repeat itself.

When Pamela Sue came to the part about him and Claire adopting Red, Lila slumped back in her chair. For once, all she had to say was one word. "Oh."

"There are problems," Claire said, drawing rings in the condensation on her water glass.

"Such as?"

"Medical ethics, for one thing."

Like Pamela Sue, Lila dismissed them with a sweep of her hand. "What else?"

"The obvious," Claire murmured under her breath.

"Ah, yes. So?" Lila prompted her.

"So, I've asked Pamela Sue to think over her decision for two weeks," Claire explained. "At the end of that time, if she hasn't changed her mind, we'll contact the authorities and begin the process of Red's adoption."

For the second time in his life, Dugan felt everything dear to him slipping through his fingers. Until Pamela Sue's announcement, he'd been willing to bet his prize bull Claire would accept the marriage proposal he planned to make after everyone else left.

Now he was sure Claire would be the first to dart out the door right after dinner. He looked over her shoulder. Outside the dining room window, the horizon glowed pink with sunset. In the sparse light, he could barely make out the plump angel marking Angela's grave.

For two wonderful days, Red had filled the void left in his heart by Angela. There'd been a time when he thought he could never look at another baby and feel the rush of pride. Yet, that emotion overwhelmed him every time he held that rascal with the lusty lungs in his arms.

His gaze drifted back to Claire. She sat there staring at him with a pitiful look on her face.

Ah, Claire, couldn't you forgive me? When push came to shove, couldn't you put the hurt behind you and trust me again?

A week had passed since Pamela Sue's and Red's homecoming. Claire had seen Dugan twice in town, but he'd only scowled at her, tipped his hat in a pretense of cordiality, and promptly ignored her. He'd stopped by to visit Pamela Sue and the baby every day. Each time he'd lingered over his good-byes as if each visit were the last.

Lila made sure Claire heard about every visit, down to the smallest of details.

After church on Sunday, Lila flitted around

her kitchen, boiling water, making formula, and telling Claire about Dugan's latest visit.

"Gunther caused quite a stir at the hospital."

Relieved to hear Lila talk about somebody besides Dugan, Claire ran her finger around the rim of her coffee cup and grinned wryly. "That doesn't surprise me. I just wish I could do more to help him."

"If the man'd helped himself, maybe you could've. Besides, look what you did for Orville. To hear him talk, you hung the moon and half the stars in the Milky Way."

"I'm glad for Orville, and I admit it feels good to know I helped him. But I still don't feel any better about Gunther."

"The way I see it, nothing on God's green earth'd make you feel better right now. Unless maybe it was a good hug from Dugan. Am I right here?"

"Maybe."

"But?"

"But when the hugging's over, the problems are still there."

"What happened out there?" Lila wanted to know. "One day I dropped off clothes for the baby, and the next I come to pick her and her momma up, and boy! I thought I'd walked into a freezer."

"Everything was going well until Pamela Sue told us about wanting to give Red up for adoption."

"What do you mean, *'everything was going well'?*"

Claire gazed into the dark liquid in her coffee cup, trying to remember only the good times at Dugan's. The way he'd assisted with Red's birth, the euphoric feeling of sharing such a miracle, their coming together again and discovering time and pain hadn't diminished their feelings for one another.

"I realized I'd never stopped loving Dugan." The bittersweet memories stuck in Claire's throat like the lump of peanut butter Lila had spread on her sandwich. "I told him so. We . . . got close. Real close."

"Then why glum city?"

"I wish I knew."

"Have you tried talkin' to him about that long face he's carryin' around?"

"He'll hardly give me the time of day."

"Well, we'll see about that."

Claire reached across the table and squeezed her aunt's hand. "Aunt Lila, stay out of this. This is none of your business."

"It is when the people I love are miserable."

"Sometimes you can't do anything about other peoples' misery."

"And sometimes you can," she maintained with a gleam in her eye that worried Claire.

"I do have something I'd appreciate your doing," Claire told her aunt.

"Just name it."

"If Pamela Sue doesn't change her mind about giving Red up for adoption, I'd appreciate it if you'd make the appropriate phone calls to set the wheels in motion."

"Me?"

Claire nodded, fighting back the tears. "I just don't think I could do it."

Lila heaved a sigh. "I know what you mean. Hardly seems right sending that sweet child away when people right here in Sierra love the little dickens."

Ten days after Claire, Pamela Sue, and Red left him in the foulest of moods, Dugan hacked away at a tree lightning had struck in the spring. In a month or so, the cold weather would settle in, and he'd appreciate the extra firewood.

Besides, he needed something to do with his hands, something to heave his weight into to diffuse the anger he couldn't shake.

While he split logs, Lazy Boy lay in the shade of the growing woodpile, his fat belly swelling rounder with age. He lifted his head and whimpered.

"What is it, boy?"

The hound dog sniffed the air and looked off to the west.

Dugan followed the direction of his gaze. A cloud of gray dust colored the western horizon.

Dugan slung his long-handled axe over his shoulder and listened for what he hoped to hear—the well-greased purr of Claire's Lincoln.

But the engine of this car was cutting out, as if it were choking. Even at a distance he could hear the telltale squeak of shocks that needed replacing.

Not Claire's sleek new Lincoln, but Lila's aging station wagon.

Well, a visit from Lila was better than nothing . . . almost.

Lila wheeled off the road, slammed on the brakes, and hopped out with the energy of a woman half her age.

"Howdy, Lila. What brings you out?"

"Stupid people."

Dugan chuckled. "Come again?"

"I said, 'stupid people.' And, my dear man, one of 'em's you."

"What have I done this time?" he asked, fending her off with open palms.

"Put your hands down. I'm not about to attack a man twice my size. What I am going to do is sit you down and have a good talk."

"About what?"

She snorted. "See, didn't I say you were stupid?"

"Lila . . ."

"Okay, okay, I'm here to talk about Claire."

"Is she okay?"

"Of course not."

"What's wrong?" he asked, hoping his pride hadn't kept him from her in a time of need.

"Her heart's breakin', that's what."

"Hers and everybody else's," he grumbled and swung his axe in a wide arc to split another log.

"If you were the smart young man I thought you were, you'd get in your pickup and drive into town and have a talk with Claire."

"About what?"

"For Pete's sake, Dugan, do I have to spell everything out for you?"

"You're talking in riddles again, Lila."

"Dugan, Dugan, where are your brains? Claire's miserable because she loves you."

"Did she tell you that?"

"She most certainly did."

"When?"

"After Pamela Sue and the baby came home."

"What else did she say?"

"That everything was going swell until Pamela Sue made her announcement. Then everything went to hell in a handbasket."

"Well put," Dugan said and pitched a split log into the stack at his side.

"Why?" Lila asked.

"I don't know. Why don't you ask Claire?"

"I did. She said to ask you! Surely one of you has an inklin' what went wrong."

"All I know is, when Pamela Sue said she wanted us—Claire and me—to adopt Red, I thought, at last our time's come. Now we can get married and have the baby both of us want. I don't mind telling you, I've carried the guilt around for years because Claire couldn't have any more children. Then providence drops a real special one right in our laps, and she freezes up and says, no thanks."

"That's what she said, 'No thanks?' "

"Same thing as."

"The way I hear it, she was worried about doctorin' ethics."

"You know as well as I do a good lawyer could cut through all that hogwash."

"You fool!"

"I — what did you call me?"

"Fool. Don't you see? Number one, Claire's busted her pretty rear end for years so she could be a doctor, and she can't do anything to risk losin' what she's worked for. Number two, before all this adoption business, she told you she loved you, and what did you do?"

"Don't you have a pretty good idea?" Dugan returned with a shuttered glance.

"I don't mean makin' love. I mean, did you pop the question?"

"No, but I was planning to, just as soon as you and Pamela Sue and Red left."

Lila clucked her tongue. "Mighty poor timin', if you ask me. That's what I'd think if I was Claire."

"I didn't want to rush her. Hell, Lila, I told her in Cancún I loved her. I've been telling her for weeks I want her to be part of my life again."

"But did you say the 'M' word?"

"Marriage?"

"Now you're gettin' the scope of it."

"Not exactly."

"Okay, we're going to play a little game here. I want you to try real hard to pretend you're Claire."

When he wanted Claire so much, stepping into her skin wouldn't be easy to do. Still, Dugan tried. "Okay."

"She loved you with all her heart, and you broke it. You sent her away."

"She said she's forgiven me for all that."

"But she can't forget it now, can she?"

"Maybe she can't, but I can't change what I've done."

"Now she swallows her pride and comes back to town so she can be Sierra's doctor, somethin' she's always wanted to do. It ain't easy. You're here. She's got powerful memories, good and bad. And all the time, you're sashayin' your tight butt around town, sayin' sweet things, touchin' her, confusin' the heck out of her."

"Go on," Dugan said, beginning to get the feel for what Claire had experienced.

"You go to Cancún. You fall in love all over again."

"I didn't have to fall in love with Claire again. I never stopped loving her."

257

"Oh, hush. Anyway, next thing you know, the two of you are out here, within sight of the very spot where Angela died, and you deliver Pamela Sue's baby. Claire's emotions are stirred up like a tornado.

"You two play house, complete with a sweet little child you can't keep your hands away from. Then all of a sudden you're as cool as a cucumber. Claire sees how much you want a baby. She knows she can't give you one. So she figures you've decided no baby, no marriage.

"You share some—" Lila cleared her throat "—mighty special moments, but still you don't ask her to marry you. Not askin' wouldn't have been no big deal if this business with Red hadn't interfered."

"Does she think I wanted to marry her just so I could be Red's daddy?"

"Wonders will never cease. Now you got the hang of it."

"Oh, Lord," Dugan muttered, cursing his insensitivity.

"She injects this doctorin' ethics into the conversation, partly because she's not about to ask you if you plan to propose. You hear what she has to say, and you assume the worst, without talkin' to her. You don't give the poor girl a chance to explain how she feels. Just like when you sent her away, Dugan, you assumed you knew what she was thinkin', without ever knowin' for sure. You made a decision you didn't have a right to make—that you and Claire could marry up so you could have Red as your own."

"And I swore I'd never do that again," Dugan said, feeling like the world's biggest louse.

"Well, I'd say you have some powerful makin' up to do."

"Can I ask you one question, Lila?" he said, a new idea buzzing around in his head.

"Shoot."

"Does she want to adopt Red?"

"Was there ever any question?"

"Okay, then," Dugan said, rubbing his fingers over his week's growth of beard. "I'll have to find a way to set things right."

"Best hurry," Lila warned him. "Only two days left till Pamela Sue makes her decision about Red. And, from the looks of things, she's got her mind fixed on givin' the little rascal up for adoption. If not to you and Claire, to some other family."

Chapter Twelve

Dugan's first impulse was to jump in his pickup and drive into Sierra, hell bent for leather.

He wanted to grab Claire and kiss her until she trembled all the way down to her toes. He didn't care if she was doctoring a patient or eating chicken fried steak at Imogene's Cafe. Afterward, he would tell her they were getting married tomorrow, and no arguments.

Which would go over like a lead balloon, damn it all! He was making another decision for Claire, assuming too much too soon, without asking how she felt.

What was he supposed to do? Romance her, then ask?

That wouldn't do. He didn't have time. Not if he wanted to give her—to give them—the chance for the baby they both desperately wanted.

He grabbed his axe, loped to the barn, and hung the tool on the wall. Hands on hips, he stood in the open doorway and surveyed the farming-ranching operation he'd built from the pitiful scrap of land his grandfather had left him.

In the pasture his prize herd of Black Angus grazed, twitching their tails at the pesky flies. The cattle had been his mainstay in drought years when crops withered in the blistering sun. Cotton dotted the fields in snowy splotches of marshmallow-white, soon to be harvested.

To the east grew sweet potatoes and peanuts, plus the small field of wheat where he'd almost lost Claire.

For years, after he sent Claire away to Philadelphia, the ranch had been his life, because he'd had no other. He admitted he'd become obsessive about lots of things—debt, for one. Watching every penny. Paying cash and trying to avoid credit like a horde of crop-crunching grasshoppers.

Now he was a man of means in most people's minds, a successful rancher, showing a profit. So many others were losing their shirts in the crunch of loan payments and government regulations.

So if he was so damned successful, why did the impressive numbers on his net worth statement mean so piddling little to him? Why was

261

the loneliness eating a hole in his gut?

Simple. Without Claire, he existed, but he didn't *live*.

Everything important to him was slipping through his fingers like a handful of dry grain.

He had to find a way to let Claire know how much she meant to him. Whether or not they could adopt Red, it was important to let her know he wanted her.

Lazy Boy, his companion through the good years and the bad, rubbed up against his leg and whimpered. He, too, sensed the impending loss.

"I'm not going to screw up this time, old boy." Dugan knelt to scratch the dog's tight, round belly. "No offense, but I don't intend to spend another twelve years moping around this place with nothing but a lazy mutt to warm my bed."

Tail thumping against the barn's dirt floor, Lazy Boy swiped his long, moist tongue over Dugan's face and smiled. Yes, that was definitely a smile creasing the folds of Lazy Boy's graying face.

Suddenly an idea popped into Dugan's exasperated brain. He stroked Lazy Boy's head and stared off into the distance, mulling over the possibilities.

"You know, boy, it just might work," he reasoned out loud. "It may cost me a bundle, but hell, what's all this worth if I can't share it with Claire?"

Recalling he'd just drained his savings account and the rest of his money was tied up in certificates of deposit, he wondered where'd he'd find the cash and find it quick.

"What the hell? I'll borrow the damned money if I have to!"

Lazy Boy took off at a fairly brisk trot. He paused to look over his shoulder. Dugan chuckled and caught up with his dog in long, determined strides.

"Don't worry, fella. I'm way ahead of you. I've got a few phone calls to make, and time's wasting. I only hope I haven't waited too long."

Claire sat at her desk for lack of something better to do on a Saturday morning, sorting through the day's meager mail, the calendar open and glaring.

Tomorrow was the day. Sunday. Two weeks. Time for Pamela Sue's final decision about the baby. No matter what the girl decided, Claire would lose the chance to raise the child she wanted so badly . . . Red.

Although Lila threw a fit every time Claire called the baby that, the name stuck. "Red" suited her looks, her already obvious temperament.

Claire opened her bottom desk drawer. With

263

loving hands, she pulled out the frilly dress she'd bought Red from Sierra's new Victorian boutique that catered to tourists. Pamela Sue wanted to hold the christening tomorrow after church. Claire promised to find just the right dress.

She fingered the antique lace that edged the sleeves and hem. The delicate gauzy fabric had been worn by another child in another christening a hundred years earlier. Red would look beautiful in the long, flowing gown.

The mental image of the baby at the ceremony plunged Claire into depression. The event could well turn out to be Red's farewell party. Claire pinched her nose between her thumb and forefinger and wept.

It wasn't fair she had to say good-bye to another infant who'd snuggled against her heart. Her vision blurring, she reached for a tissue. She couldn't soil the christening outfit with tears of sadness. Today, though, was the time to weep. Tomorrow she should be all smiles for Red's special day.

Go to him. Tell him you want to marry him. Save yourself this grief.

No. No matter how much she wanted to mother that sweet, precious child, Red couldn't be the reason for Claire and Dugan to remarry.

Even if they could risk failure again, she couldn't do that to Pamela Sue's baby. The child deserved parents who were committed first to each other. That strength would sustain their marriage in lean, troubled times.

Claire folded the fragile garment and tucked it back in the drawer. She'd promised the decorators she'd take a look at the ceramic tile samples they'd left at the house for her to look over. She'd cancelled the Dallas connection and hired both the locals, as Dugan had suggested

The tile was fine. The floors were fine. Everything about her new house was fine. She didn't care anymore.

Arms crossed over her chest, Claire wandered about upstairs, her footsteps echoing on the hardwood floors. These empty rooms would never echo with the laughter of a delighted child or the impassioned cries of Dugan and her making love.

How she missed him! The coziness of his bedroom as they romped and teased and soared to the heights of heaven.

A familiar gravelly voice echoed up the wooden stairwell. "Miss Claire? Claire?"

She leaned over the railing and yelled, "Fred, is that you?"

"Yes, ma'am."

Claire waved him up. He was a welcome sight in her lonely house. "Come on up. I'll give you a grand tour."

"Not that I don't appreciate the offer but

I've got to be gettin' back to the hotel. We're expectin' a family in from Dallas any minute. They'll be needin' help with their bags."

"Later maybe," Claire said, descending the stairs to give Fred a big hug.

"I came to deliver a message."

"Does someone need to see me at the clinic?"

"Someone needs to see you all right, but not at the clinic. Here." He handed Claire a sheet of hotel stationery on which the owner had scribbled a short note.

Must see you at the ranch. Twelve o'clock. Don't be late. Dugan. With a P.S. at the bottom. *Important clinic business.*

She frowned at the impersonal nature of the note. Is this what their relationship had deteriorated to? Terse memos about business?

She ran her thumb over the words and gazed east out the beveled glass of the dining room window. A gentle breeze ruffled leaves over recently sodded lawn. The green turf could cushion Red's scrambling feet if only Claire would compromise.

"You miss him, don't you?" Fred was saying.

"Hmm?"

"You know — Dugan."

Claire exhaled his name in a deeply drawn breath. "Dugan." She lowered her lashes. "Yes. I'm afraid I do."

266

"It's just like you never came back."

"What do you mean?"

"He's mopin' around, grumpy as a bear with a thorn in his paw. Least he was till yesterday. He came speedin' into town and sprung up the stairs to Orville's bank, coiled up tighter'n a rattlesnake."

"I wonder what that was all about?"

"Beats me. But I'll tell you what, Miss Claire. Folks around here'd appreciate it if you'd put him out of his misery."

Claire felt her cheeks grow hot at the implication of Fred's statement. "I hardly think—"

"Now, don't go gettin' your back up. I didn't mean *that*."

"What did you mean?"

"Durned if I know for sure, but maybe when you see him today you'll figure it out."

"I wonder why he didn't drive in and talk to me here?"

"No tellin'. Well, got to get back. Tell Dugan I said howdy."

With the day as summery warm as mid-June, Claire changed into her pink sundress for her appointment with Dugan.

In a couple of weeks, fall would chase these days from Sierra, along with Claire's chance to wear the clothes she'd splurged on in Cancún.

Dugan would probably think she dressed in the off-the-shoulder dress for him. So what? She had a right to look soft and feminine in her off-duty hours, didn't she?

By the time she wheeled into Dugan's long, narrow driveway that logic escaped her. She felt foolish dressed as if she and Dugan were about to step out on a date.

She supposed that feeling would pass in time. She'd settle into a routine of living in Sierra without thinking of Dugan making love to her every time she slipped in and out of her clothes.

"And pigs might fly." She grumbled one of Lila's famous declarations. She scooted out of her car and smoothed her hands over the long, full skirt on her way to the door of Dugan's house.

She lifted her hand to knock, then hesitated. There, tucked into the door's screen was a white scrap of paper with her name on it. After coping with all the butterflies flitting around in her stomach, if Dugan had changed his mind about their appointment, she would be as mad as a banty hen.

Meet me out back, the note read. *Dugan.*

Well, good. He hadn't wandered off. She tamped down the uncalled-for irritation and headed for the side of the house. He was probably tinkering in the barn. She remembered he used to spend his Saturdays there, grooming the horses and cleaning the farm implements.

She also remembered on days as beautiful as this more than once she had brought Dugan his lunch, and they had wound up making love in the hayloft.

A muscle low in her abdomen ticked. How she would savor making love to Dugan right now. But apparently that wasn't to be, or Dugan wouldn't have avoided her for almost two weeks.

After she'd left with Lila, Pamela Sue and Red, he'd probably thought long and hard and made some decisions. Likely he'd finally realized that wanting Claire back after all those years had been more fantasy than reality.

Feeling more foolish than ever for wearing the deep V-necked sundress, Claire contemplated running back to the hotel to change. "To hell with it." She was here. She would see Dugan. They would conduct their business and be done with it.

Her chin lifted in a bolstering resolve, she rounded the corner of the house and almost fainted.

There he was, sitting behind the wheel of Old Ruby, smiling and tipping his dress felt hat in a gentlemanly greeting. He looked for all the world like that handsome young man she'd fallen in love with when she was fifteen.

Lord, what was happening? Why was he in that truck, and where were the sunflowers that had shot through the rusted-out holes in Ruby's flat bed?

Old Ruby roared to life with a spit, a sputter and a shimmy. Dugan waved her over with a gesture of his open hand. She realized she'd been standing there, gawking at him as if she were a shy teenager. She shook off that ridiculous expression and strode across the lawn to see what Dugan wanted.

"Hi, Doc," he said, arms folded across the steering wheel.

"Hi, Dugan."

"You look awful pretty."

"Thank you. I understand we have business to discuss."

"Yep. You want to hop in?" He reached across the passenger seat and opened the door. "I'd get out and help you, but I'm afraid Ruby might stall if I do."

"Why don't we just discuss our business here?"

"I'm a bit strapped for time. Come on. You don't mind, do you?"

"Well, okay." She climbed onto the seat and shut the door with a hard yank, wondering if Dugan was as intensely aware of her as she was of him.

She turned and saw that his dimple plunged deep into his cheek. The rat was up to some sort of devilishness. What had he dreamed up and what did it have to do with the clinic?

"Thought we'd go for a picnic."

"To talk business?"

"Yep." He pumped the accelerator. Ruby shook, coughed, then lurched onto the dirt path leading to the south forty. "Have you had lunch?"

"Well, no."

"Great. Imogene called this morning long about seven to tell me she'd cooked up a big batch of fried chicken and potato salad, so I told her to save me some. I figured we might as well eat while we're talking."

Dugan worn a clean pair of faded jeans and the belt of soft brown leather she'd painstakingly tooled "Nichols" on as a wedding present. And he still had the white Western shirt she'd practically ripped off his body the first time they'd made love after Red's birth.

Dugan down-shifted Ruby. Claire's gaze skimmed over his hard, muscled thighs and stopped at his boots. He'd worn the black ones, the same pair he'd sported at their wedding. They had been polished until they gleamed.

My, but he looked handsome!

The aroma of Imogene's fried chicken wafted past Claire's nose.

She was hungry, and yet the moment she caught sight of Dugan in Old Ruby her stomach had tied into knots. How could she eat when all the feelings—the love—came rushing

271

at her like a herd of stampeding cattle? When simply riding in Old Ruby made the insides of her thighs crave the touch of Dugan's caressing fingers?

"Where are we going?" she asked.

"Up ahead a spell. Could you give me a hand here?"

"What do you want me to do?"

"Actually I need your foot." He braked to a halt at the fence to Joseph Witcomb's north forty. "Keep giving her the gas, will you? I'll be right back."

Dugan hopped from the cab, unhooked the crossed-timber gate and swung it open. In seconds they were jostling down the weed-covered trail in Joseph's pasture.

Suddenly Claire knew exactly where they were going. How could Dugan do this to her?

"Stop the truck," she demanded.

"Why?" he asked, bringing the pickup to a halt anyway.

"I-I don't want to go where you're taking me."

"Ah, Claire. Don't be so uptight. We're just going to have a picnic."

"But why there?" she demanded to know, indicating with a nod of her head an all-too-familiar spot beside the stream.

"Simple. Best place around to have a picnic." Dugan hopped down from the cab.

Claire stayed glued to the seat, letting her

senses soak in the place and the memories. Clear water still tumbled over rocks in the narrow stream that snaked through the pasture. Overhead jets from Reese Air Force Base in Lubbock streaked white contrails across the brilliant blue sky. Beneath an oak tree Joseph had nurtured over the years, Dugan snapped his grandmother's quilt in the air, then spread it neatly on the flat ground.

All about them the last wildflowers of summer exploded in an attempt to procreate— pinks and violets and buttercup yellows. A light breeze caressed Claire's face and ruffled her hair.

She closed her eyes and smelled hay, the hint of wildflowers and . . . Dugan.

She popped open her eyes. He stood beside the truck, his arms folded over the open window, tanned and bare where he'd rolled up his sleeves. His eyes were warm brown and fixed on her face. "You going to eat in there?"

He tugged on the handle, brooking no refusal. The door swung open. He offered her his hand. Gingerly she placed her palm in his. If only they could act out her dreams, her time-held fantasies.

No. Dugan had asked her to his ranch for a business lunch. She would have to act accordingly.

Dugan, however, didn't seem like he had business on his mind. He reclined on his side of the quilt, head propped in his hand, and studied her.

Unnerved by the intensity of his gaze, she reached for the picnic basket and flipped up the lid. She had to find something to do with her hands. Otherwise she might lose her mind and rake her fingers through the springy chest hair visible through the opening of his shirt.

While Dugan's lips curved into a disconcerting, teasing smile, she dished up potato salad on the red plastic plates. For Dugan, a helping large enough to choke a horse, the way she remembered he liked it. For her, a single spoonful.

"On a diet?"

"No."

"You sick?"

"I'm feeling well, thank you."

"You're eating like a bird."

"I-I'm not very hungry."

"But you said you hadn't eaten lunch."

"Dugan . . . please." She took a bite of a crispy chicken breast that went down her throat like a wadded-up sock. "What was it you wanted to talk about?"

Dugan dropped his gaze and focused unsmiling on the drumstick in his hand. "Come to think of it, I'm not so hungry myself." He plunked the chicken on his plate, tossed it in the picnic basket and glanced away for a long, silent moment.

Beside them, not five feet away, the water trickled over smooth rocks. Claire thought of the powerful surf that had nipped at their feet that last night on the beach.

Somewhere in the distance a horse whinnied. The sun heated the bare skin of her shoulders. Yet, warmed as she was by the weather, and by Dugan's presence, a shiver snaked up her spine and scattered goose bumps down her arms.

He propped his forearms on bent knees and dangled his hands in between. It was the same space where Claire had tucked her leg when they'd snuggled in his bed only two weeks ago.

"Claire," he began, no dimple in his cheek now, only eyes boring into her, serious and searching.

"Yes?"

"I didn't come here to talk about the clinic."

"But you said—"

"I lied. I didn't think you'd make the trip out here if I told you the truth."

"What is the truth then, Dugan?"

"I've got a lot to say, and I don't want you to interrupt me until I'm through."

Hope was springing up in jillions of spots in her alert body. She smoothed her hands over her skirt. "Fair enough."

"For starters, Claire . . ." he reached over and tucked a strand of hair behind her ear

". . . I love you. More than I've ever loved anyone in my life."

"Sometimes love isn't—"

He pressed the pad of his forefinger to her lips and told her in a husky voice, "Shh. You promised."

She nodded.

"And if you're sure you've forgiven me for sending you away when I should have slung you over my shoulder and made you go live with Lila a while, I'd be honored if you'd be my wife . . . again."

The whole world was spinning at a dizzying speed, only Claire sat there, unmoving. "If you're asking because of Red—"

This time Dugan silenced her with his lips. The kiss was tender, chaste, and oh so tempting. "Only this time I'll do it right. I'll stand by you, I swear I will, Claire."

He took her hand and squeezed it tight between his fingers.

What could Claire say to make him understand? Only what was in her heart, she decided. "I love you, too, Dugan, but—"

He tugged on her hand, and she leaned into his welcoming kiss. "No buts." He kissed her again, this time grinning.

"Stop it, Dugan. Stop pretending everything's okay."

"What isn't okay?"

"You're doing it again. You're asking me to

276

marry you for—for convenience. Yes, that's it. For a reason."

"The reason is because I love you."

"No, the reason is you want to adopt Red," Claire flung at him.

"That, my dear lady, is where you're dead wrong."

"Then why didn't you ask me to marry you before Pamela Sue told us she wanted us to adopt Red? You had all weekend. You told me in Cancún you wanted to get married again, but you wouldn't unless I could forgive you . . . unless you knew I loved you."

"For Pete's sake, if you'd given me time, I'd have asked."

"How am I supposed to believe that?"

"I was going to after Lila came to take Pamela Sue and Red back to town. But you never gave me the chance. You just sat there and made excuses why you couldn't adopt Red. I thought, hell, she doesn't want to marry me. It was all in her mind. Now that she knows she can have me, she doesn't want me. Her wanting was all in her mind and body, not in her heart."

Claire pressed her fingertips to her temples. What Dugan was saying made sense, yet she was so afraid to believe it. "I saw you with Red. I saw how much you liked her. I could tell how much you want a baby and I knew I couldn't give you one.

"After Red was born, you acted funny. Distant. Like a light bulb flashed in your head and you realized what you'd really wanted all along was children. Then, when Pamela Sue said Red could be ours, you suddenly decided I'd fit in the picture. You sat there talking like you assumed we'd get married, but you didn't ask. You just said, we've got a few problems to work out first.

"I thought, here he goes again, making my decisions for me. I wanted to scream, 'Ask me! Ask me if I'll marry you.' But you didn't."

"I'm asking you now, Claire."

"Oh, Dugan, I don't know. What if you're confused about your feelings? I can't bear to think of you sending me away again."

"I thought you might say that, so I came prepared." He strode to the truck, reached through the open window, and pounded a fist against the dashboard. The glove box fell open. Claire heard him slam it shut, then watched him return and lower himself to the quilt with a large envelope in his hand.

"Here," he said and handed it to her.

"What is this?"

"Legal papers."

"For what?"

"Red's adoption."

"But Pamela Sue isn't announcing her decision until tomorrow."

278

"She did that two weeks ago. You just wouldn't listen. She hasn't changed her mind, Claire. She wants to give Red a good home and get on with her own life."

"But—"

"You've got three choices, all yours, all legal. I hired a lawyer. He checked his books, even talked to a judge. There'd be some paperwork other than what's in that envelope. You'd have to go before the judge and say your piece. But you delivering Red won't get in the way of adopting her."

"You hired a lawyer to research this?"

He nodded, a proud glint in his eyes.

"That must have cost a lot of money."

"Sure did."

"I thought all your cash was tied up."

"I borrowed it, okay?"

A smile crept across Claire's face. "You took out a loan to pay for the attorney?"

"He wanted his fee, up front."

Claire knew what a sacrifice going into debt must have been for Dugan. "You said I have three choices," she prompted him, hope flickering in her chest. "What are they?"

"One, you can marry me, and we'll adopt Red. The papers are there in that envelope."

"Or?"

"You can marry me, and we won't adopt Red. An agency will find another family.

"Three, you can tell me you don't want to

be my wife, and . . ." his eyes turned a deep shade of brown ". . . you can adopt Red all by yourself."

"You arranged that for me?"

"Yep." He tapped the envelope. "Papers're right there."

"Pamela Sue agreed?"

"Yep again."

Claire looked deep into Dugan's eyes and saw the hurt there, the loneliness and the wanting that matched hers. He didn't want to give her up or Red. He wanted them together, as a family. More than anything, though, he wanted her happiness. And, he wasn't forcing any decisions on her this time.

"I never thought—" she began.

"If it's all the same with you, I'd just as soon you not start your answer with that never word."

Claire grinned and reached her hand across the quilt to squeeze his. "I was going to say, I never thought my heart could feel like it was going to burst again." She pressed their joined hands over her thumping heart and sighed deeply.

"Does that mean yes?" he asked hesitantly, not moving his fingers.

"It means yes."

He narrowed his gaze. "To which question?"

"I'll be your wife, Dugan, and that little rascal's mother."

Dugan let out a war whoop and pulled Claire into his arms. Before she could utter another word, he jumped to his feet and spun her around. She clung to Dugan for dear life and for the love of him.

Then suddenly his lips were on hers. He sank to the quilt with Claire still in his arms. "The way I see it," he said, a merry twinkle in his eye and his dimple deep in his cheek, "we ought to seal this agreement."

He lowered his head and captured her lips in a deep, soul-thirsty kiss before adding, "and with more than a kiss, my wife-to-be. With more than a kiss."

Epilogue

The entire town of Sierra turned out for Red's christening. At Pamela Sue's request, the event was held outdoors in a tree-shaded courtyard behind the church.

Fred, teary-eyed, blew his bulbous nose into a white handkerchief. Orville and Ruthie Garrison stood hand in hand and wistfully admired Sierra's newest citizen. Before the ceremony Orville slipped Claire a savings passbook, showing a thousand dollar deposit in the auspicious name of Red Nichols.

Claire let her gaze drift over the crowd, loving every one of the town's residents, even though a few had yet to completely warm to her return. She only wished Gunther could have joined them. When she'd phoned the doctor directing the emphysema research study in Lubbock, he'd sighed and muttered he didn't think Gunter would live long enough to make the trip.

While the minister sprinkled water over the infant's bawling head, Claire and Dugan stood nearby, arm in arm, grinning at the screwed-up face that matched her name — Red.

She would not be slight of character or fortitude. She had already demonstrated by her lusty voice and night-owlish nature she intended to exert her will in this world. Her proud parents-to-be, sure she was gifted and talented and would most certainly be a future governor of Texas, if not the President of the United States, wholeheartedly agreed.

Dugan's foreman and his fiancé, the proud godparents, did their best to jiggle Red until the ceremony's conclusion. Then Auntie Lila whisked her away to a fresh bottle, a rocker and a wet, reassuring lick from Lazy Boy's tongue.

Pamela Sue watched in rapt silence, periodically dabbing at her eyes with a Battenburg lace handkerchief Claire had given her as a remembrance of the occasion.

"She's one lucky little girl," Pamela Sue said, lips trembling, as Lila pressed a now-placid child smelling sweetly of milk into Claire's arms.

Dugan wrapped his arm around the teenager's shoulders and let her sob against the whiteness of his shirt. "I know how you feel, giving her up."

"Like someone stabbed me in the chest."

"Exactly."

"But it's best for her — and me."

"You know where she'll be. You can drop in

anytime. We're going to raise Red knowing who her birth momma is."

"I-I won't intrude. She deserves a peaceful life with you and Dr. Linwood."

"I'm not sure how peaceful life will be with Red," Claire joked and handed the squirming bundle of gauzy cotton and lace up to Dugan's shoulder.

"Have you decided where you're going to live?" Pamela Sue asked.

Claire glanced up into Dugan's eyes and smiled with the radiance of a woman who'd reconnected with the one man who could make her life complete. After they'd made love by the stream yesterday, they'd decided on their living arrangements. "Sometimes in town. Sometimes on the farm."

Pamela Sue sighed. "Lucky girl. Two houses."

"Homes," Dugan corrected.

"When's the wedding?"

"Next weekend."

"So soon?"

Claire and Dugan exchanged hot glances. "The way we see it," Claire explained as she slipped her arm around Dugan and hugged the man she'd loved all her life, "we feel lucky in love. There's no reason on God's green earth to wait any longer to renew the ties that bind."

CATCH A RISING STAR!

ROBIN ST. THOMAS

FORTUNE'S SISTERS   (2616, $3.95)
It was Pia's destiny to be a Hollywood star. She had complete
self-confidence, breathtaking beauty, and the help of her domi-
neering mother. But her younger sister Jeanne began to steal the
spotlight meant for Pia, diverting attention away from the ruth-
lessly ambitious star. When her mother Mathilde started to return
the advances of dashing director Wes Guest, Pia's jealousy surfaced. Her passion for Guest and desire to be the brightest star in
Hollywood pitted Pia against her own family—sister against sister, mother against daughter. Pia was determined to be the only
survivor in the arenas of love and fame. But neither Mathilde nor
Jeanne would surrender without a fight. . . .

LOVER'S MASQUERADE   (2886, $4.50)
New Orleans. A city of secrets, shrouded in mystery and magic.
A city where dreams become obsessions and memories once again
become reality. A city where even one trip, like a stop on Claudia
Gage's book promotion tour, can lead to a perilous fall. For New
Orleans is also the home of Armand Dantine, who knows the secrets that Claudia would conceal and the past she cannot remember. And he will stop at nothing to make her love him, and will
not let her go again . . .

SENSATION   (3228, $4.95)
They'd dreamed of stardom, and their dreams came true. Now
they had fame and the power that comes with it. In Hollywood,
in New York, and around the world, the names of Aurora Styles,
Rachel Allenby, and Pia Decameron commanded immediate attention—and lust and envy as well. They were stars, idols on ped-
estals. And there was always someone waiting in the wings to
bring them crashing down . . .

*Available wherever paperbacks are sold, or order direct from the
Publisher. Send cover price plus 50¢ per copy for mailing and
handling to Zebra Books, Dept. 3840, 475 Park Avenue South,
New York, N.Y. 10016. Residents of New York and Tennessee
must include sales tax. DO NOT SEND CASH. For a free Zebra/
Pinnacle catalog please write to the above address.*

OFFICIAL ENTRY FORM
Please enter me in the

Lucky in Love

SWEEPSTAKES

Grand Prize choice: _____

Name: _____

Address: _____

City: _____ **State** _____ **Zip** _____

Store name: _____

Address: _____

City: _____ **State** _____ **Zip** _____

MAIL TO: LUCKY IN LOVE
P.O. Box 1022B
Grand Rapids, MN 55730-1022B

Sweepstakes ends: 3/31/93

OFFICIAL RULES
"LUCKY IN LOVE" SWEEPSTAKES

1. To enter complete the official entry form. No purchase necessary. You may enter by hand printing on a 3″ x 5″ piece of paper, your name, address and the words "Lucky In Love." Mail to: "Lucky In Love" Sweepstakes, P.O. Box 1022B, Grand Rapids, MN 55730-1022-B.

2. Enter as often as you like, but each entry must be mailed separately. Mechanically reproduced entries not accepted. Entries must be received by March 31, 1993.

3. Winners selected in a random drawing on or about April 16, 1993 from among all eligible entries received by Marden-Kane, Inc. an independent judging organization whose decisions are final and binding. Winner may be required to sign an affidavit of eligibility and release which must be returned within 14 days or alternate winner(s) will be selected. Winners permit the use of their name/photograph for publicity/advertising purposes without further compensation. No transfer of prizes permitted. Taxes are the sole responsibility of the prize winners. Only one prize per family or household.

4. Winners agree that the sponsor, its affiliate and their agencies and employees shall not be liable for injury, loss or damage of any kind resulting from participation in this promotion or from the acceptance or use of the prizes awarded.

5. Sweepstakes open to residents of the U.S., except employees of Zebra Books, their affiliates, advertising and promotion agencies and Marden-Kane, Inc. Void where taxed, prohibited or restricted by law. All Federal, State and Local laws and regulations apply. Odds of winning depend upon the total number of eligible entries received. All prizes will be awarded. Not responsible for lost, misdirected mail or printing errors.

6. For the name of the Grand Prize Winner, send a self-addressed stamped envelope to: "Lucky In Love" Winners, P.O. Box 706-B, Sayreville, NJ 08871.